Things
Seen
from
Above

Also by Shelley Pearsall

THINGS Seen FROM Above

Shelley Pearsall

illustrated by
Xingye Jin

ALFRED A. KNOPF

New York

Text copyright © 2020 by Shelley Pearsall
Jacket art copyright © 2020 by Becca Clason
Interior illustrations copyright © 2020 by Xingye Jin

All rights reserved. Published in the United States by Alfred A. Knopf,
an imprint of Random House Children's Books,
a division of Penguin Random House LLC, New York.

Knopf, Borzoi Books, and the colophon are registered trademarks
of Penguin Random House LLC.

Visit us on the Web! rhcbooks.com

Educators and librarians, for a variety of teaching tools, visit us at RHTeachersLibrarians.com

Library of Congress Cataloging-in-Publication Data is available upon request.
ISBN 978-1-5247-1739-1 (trade) — ISBN 978-1-5247-1740-7 (lib. bdg.) —
ISBN 978-1-5247-1741-4 (ebook)

The text of this book is set in 12-point Horley Old Style and 12.5-point Sassoon Sans.
Interior design by Trish Parcell

Printed in the United States of America
February 2020
10 9 8 7 6 5 4 3 2 1

First Edition

Random House Children's Books
supports the First Amendment and celebrates the right to read.

FOR MILES

What you see depends not only on what you look at, but also, where you look from.

—JAMES DEACON

April: What Am I Doing Here?

Joey Byrd looked like he was dead.

I'm not joking.

Pretty much everybody at Marshallville Elementary knew who Joey Byrd was.

You could be walking to lunch or gym class, and suddenly you'd notice this pale-haired boy lying flat on the hallway tiles—arms out, eyes closed—as if he'd just been struck by a bolt of lightning. Usually a teacher would be standing nearby trying to coax him to get up and motioning for everyone else to go around, saying, "Just ignore him. Keep moving."

But today, Joey Byrd was lying in the middle of the playground, only a few feet away from where I was sitting. It was only my second day as a Buddy Bench volunteer. I had no idea whether I should go and get Mrs. Zeff, the recess aide, or not. She seemed like a nice lady, but she also seemed pretty frazzled.

Fortunately, Marshallville's playground wasn't hard blacktop—it was wood chips. And also fortunately, it was a sunny and warm day for the first week of September in Michigan.

Still, I figured the little kid had to be really uncomfortable with all of those pointy pieces of bark sticking in his back while ants, and who knows what else, crawled all over him. . . .

Actually, he hadn't budged since recess started.

I checked the time on my phone. Fifteen minutes had already gone by. His arms had stayed frozen in place—angled diagonally from his sides. His eyes were closed. If you'd drawn a white line around him, he would've looked like one of those police outlines of a dead body.

Was he thinking? Pouting? In some kind of trance?

The day before, he'd walked around a tree all recess. I'm serious. Our playground had only one tree—a kind of scraggly maple tree—donated by the class of 2003. Everybody called it the 2003 Tree. Joey had spent about thirty minutes of yesterday's recess walking around it, making larger and larger circles in the wood chips with his left sneaker. I had no idea why. It had made me dizzy just watching him.

Today, my eyes kept going over to him automatically as I sat on the Buddy Bench. I couldn't help it—I had to keep checking that he was okay. Luckily, his pink eyelids fluttered and clenched against the bright sunlight, and his fingertips moved a little in the dirt, so that's how I knew he was still alive.

Finally, I got up from the bench and tried to talk to him.

"Hey, you've been lying there for a long time," I said in this super-cheerful voice. "Are you okay?"

The boy's pale face scrunched into a grimace, and he crossed his arms over his chest like an annoyed mummy, so I knew he'd heard me. But he didn't open his eyes and he didn't answer. Sighing, I went back to the Buddy Bench.

What am I doing here? I wondered.

My eyes flickered toward the motionless form again. *What was he doing here?*

Reaching for the notebook I'd brought outside, I jotted those questions on a back page. The questions seemed simple, but I had a feeling the answers would take much longer to find.

JOEYBYRD

Joey loved turning things around in his mind and looking at them from above. Like a bird. Like his last name, Byrd.

From above, the playground of Marshallville Elementary looked like a small, earth-colored square in a huge quilt. Around the school you could see the different patterns of the sports fields, parking lots, and neighborhoods. The hazy cluster of buildings in the distance were Kellogg's factories where they made breakfast cereal for America.

Sometimes the air smelled like cornflakes.

If you zoomed in, you might notice a bright blue bench in the middle of the playground with a skinny tree not too far away from it.

There were other things scattered around the edges of the space—two old swing sets, a small slide, and a rusty jungle gym—but the blue bench was the most visible detail by far.

Everyone called it the Buddy Bench. Joey didn't know why. The bench didn't have any buddies. It was the only one.

Although Joey's eyes were closed, he could tell that someone was sitting on the bench watching him. He had seen her before. She was from the older grades and she had straight brown hair and glasses. Today she was holding a notebook on her lap.

From above, the notebook looked like an empty white rectangle.

Joey didn't know who the girl was, or why she was sitting there during the fourth-grade recess, but he had a feeling it meant something in his life was about to change.

April: Green Chickens

So why was I sitting by myself on a Popsicle-blue bench trying to be a buddy to fourth graders?

I put most of the blame on my (former) friend Julie Vanderbrook and what had happened on the first day of sixth grade. But maybe it had started long before that. If I'm being honest, I've never had a lot of friends, mostly because I'm not interested in all the gossip and social stuff. And I'm not good at pretending I am.

Julie and I had been friends since the middle of fourth grade, when both of us got glasses during the same week. Plus, we were in the same higher-level math and reading classes together. That's how our friendship started.

Even back then, she had more friends and was more social than me. I just followed along, figuring our friendship would continue forever—because, well, why wouldn't it?

Anyway, I hadn't seen Julie much during the summer before sixth grade. (Okay, not at all.) She texted me a couple of times at the beginning of summer vacation and I texted her back. That was it.

Honestly, I didn't think it was that big of a deal—both of us were busy with camps and family stuff. And our summer vacation was really short. Unlike a lot of school districts in Michigan, we always started the third week of August.

But when I saw Julie on our first day back after summer break, I was kind of shocked by how much she had changed. Maybe I looked different too. My hair was slightly longer than usual. It was almost touching my shoulders, and I had new reddish-framed glasses, and I was wearing these obviously new sneakers that my mom had convinced me to get for school and now I seriously regretted. . . .

But Julie seemed to have gone into a maturity time machine and turned into a totally different person.

As she strolled over to say hello to me in the hallway, it took me a minute to realize the biggest change—Julie's glasses were missing. And I was pretty sure she was wearing contacts and eye makeup because her eyes seemed to be bigger or darker or something.

Plus, she had on these stylish shorts and a tight lime-green T-shirt and one small section of her straight blond hair had been dyed with a streak of bright pink.

I tried to keep my face from giving away how shocked I felt.

When she got to where I was standing, Julie rammed her shoulder into mine and said, "Hey, stranger. What's up?" Then she lowered her voice. "Green chickens, pass it on."

I had no clue what she was talking about, so I said, "What?"

Then Julie burst out laughing and said, "Oh, I guess you don't know, do you?"

Clearly, I didn't.

That day, things only continued to get worse. After homeroom, Julie switched from her assigned locker to one that was near some of the jocks. At lunch, she wanted to sit with a group of the semi-popular girls who spent the whole time throwing French fries at each other. Sitting on the other side of Julie, I spent most of lunch pretend-laughing at how (not) funny this was.

The next day, Julie sat with the same group, and I took the same spot again—which I know sounds dumb, but I wasn't sure what else to do.

Usually I had no idea what the inside joke of the day was about. Green chickens, orange slushies, potato chip penalties—what did they mean?

And you could never predict what would happen at lunch either. You could get harassed about what you brought for lunch, or what weird style jeans you were wearing, or even the fact that your cell phone case had rhinestones on it.

Mine did. And I still had no clue what significant and embarrassing thing it meant. My mom had made it for my birthday in June, so I couldn't just make it disappear without hurting her feelings.

Most of the time, Julie didn't seem to notice (or care) that I was at her table, but I was afraid she would *definitely* notice if I moved somewhere else. That was my dilemma. To move or not to move?

One lunch period, the drama was all about who was daring (or stupid) enough to write the name of a boy they liked—okay, wanted to ask out—in permanent marker on the bottom of their shoes. You were supposed to walk around all day without anybody seeing it. All the girls at my lunch table did it.

Trying to stay out of everything, I wrote the name William S. in tiny letters on my shoe and told everybody it was a boy I liked at another school.

"No way. I don't believe you," Julie scoffed, with one of her usual arm smacks. "Where did you meet him?"

"Camp this summer." It wasn't exactly a lie. I'd done a three-day arts camp where we'd studied William Shakespeare and watched some college actors present a scene from *Hamlet*. They had been really good, actually.

"Show me a picture," Julie insisted.

That's when I decided I had to leave. Because the drama was getting worse by the hour.

I applied for the Buddy Bench job because being a buddy meant you gave up your own lunch period to help out with the younger grades. Convenient, right? Sixth graders didn't have recess at Marshallville—we had an activity block at the end of the day for sports and academic stuff, so I only had to worry about escaping from lunch.

On my application, I described how the job would help with understanding others (or *avoiding* them, in my case). And I talked about how it would give me more material for the advice column I wrote for our school newspaper each month.

Our paper was called *The Tiger Times*, but it was more like a newsletter than a newspaper. My section was called April's Advice Box, and kids left questions for me using an actual box in the intermediate hallway.

The box was painted orange with black paw prints on the sides, and there was a slot in the top for questions. My mom had helped me design it.

I usually chose one or two questions from the box to answer in the newspaper each month. Last year some of my topics had been serious things like *dealing with parents getting divorced* or *how to be a better friend* . . . ironic, right? Others had been sillier, like whether hamsters or iguanas make better pets. (Yes, someone asked me that.)

When I started the column in fifth grade, I honestly thought it would help me seem more open and friendly, and well . . . *normal.* I liked to write, and I thought the box idea used my weird last name, Boxler, in a fun way.

What I didn't consider was the fact that normal kids don't usually write advice columns for other kids, and it would only reinforce the idea that I thought I was smarter and better than everybody else. (Which isn't true, but I've basically given up trying to change people's minds.)

And, of course, it didn't take long before I started getting called "the Box" by some of the obnoxious people in my grade.

Sometimes I wished I was better at seeing the drawbacks of my own ideas before I tried them.

Like the Buddy Bench job, for instance.

Although it seemed like a good idea at the time, the first week ended up being a lot harder than I thought it would be. The fourth graders didn't respect my age and listen to me like I thought they would. I hated wearing the official Buddy Bench shirt, which was school-bus yellow and said I'M YOUR BUDDY on the back in large black letters. And Joey kept walking in circles and lying down and worrying me.

By Friday I had filled an entire page of my notebook about him.

JOEYBYRD

Most people didn't know this interesting fact, but the Australian wedge-tailed eagle (*Aquila audax*) had possibly the best eyesight among all the birds in the world. Its eyes could zoom in and out to see things close-up or far away. *Aquila audax* could also fly higher than some drones.

Joey often pictured himself as an eagle.

Sometimes he forgot he wasn't one.

From an eagle's point of view, the sports fields of Marshallville Elementary looked like a giant green game board covered with colorful, moving dots. The dots were Joey's classmates, of course. But the great thing was that the kids who were weak and puny looked exactly the same as the ones who were tough and sporty. You couldn't tell them apart.

Since Joey was smaller than most fourth graders—and not sporty at all—he liked this viewpoint a lot.

But it was also impossible to tell the difference between enemies and friends.

Joey had learned this lesson the hard way. He'd learned that if you wanted to protect yourself—or be left alone—the best thing to do was lie down. From above, this made you look much larger—and most people, except teachers, would go away.

Another thing Joey had learned:

From above, the insides of most things were a mystery. Which meant Joey usually had to guess about them. He often guessed wrong. So things like sandwiches and people were mysteries to Joey. He couldn't figure them out.

But the top of a pizza was easy.

Sometimes he wished the world were more like a pizza.

April: Daydreaming with Your Eyes Closed

"So how did it go this week?"

This was the first question Mr. MacArthur (otherwise known as Mr. Mac) asked our Buddy Bench group on Friday. He was the guidance counselor at Marshallville, and he ran the Buddy Bench program. We sat around the table in his small office after school, sharing a bag of half-burned microwave popcorn.

I was surprised that there were only four students at the meeting, including me. In the past, it seemed like there had been a ton of Buddy Bench volunteers from the sixth grade. Hadn't anyone else applied?

The two other sixth graders at the table didn't exactly fill me with joy either. Although they weren't in any of my classes this year, I knew who they were. They'd been virtually inseparable since first grade. Everyone—including the teachers—called them the two Rs.

Rochelle Dobbins was loud and pushy (and, I'd like to point out, she once stole markers from me back in kindergarten). Rachel Tallentine was her ever-present dark shadow who favored black everything—nail polish, T-shirts, sneakers . . . you name it. Fortunately, they had been assigned to an earlier recess than mine because they had a different lunch.

At the opposite end of the table was a fifth grader who looked completely petrified. She was a new student from India. Apparently, Mr. Mac had just recruited her because he needed more volunteers.

"This is Veena," Mr. Mac said cheerfully. "She came all the way from India to check out what Marshallville is like, right?"

Looking embarrassed, the girl nodded slightly.

"I invited her to join us and see what the Buddy Bench is all about," Mr. Mac added.

I was convinced the girl wouldn't last very long. She was the size of a third grader. Her eyes blinked nervously behind a pair of round aqua frames. She seemed so shy that she could barely manage to smile.

"Okay, so how did it go this week?" Mr. Mac asked again, since nobody had jumped in to answer his first question yet.

The two Rs each grabbed another handful of popcorn and chewed loudly, saying nothing. The girl from India stared at her folded hands on the table.

Feeling self-conscious, I glanced down at my notebook—the one where I'd jotted down all my Buddy Bench observations and questions from the week. Of course, no one else had a notebook in front of them. No one else looked as if they'd even *thought* of bringing a notebook.

Rochelle and Rachel noticed and smirked at each other.

"Go on, April." Mr. Mac gave one of his goofy grins. "Don't be shy. Why don't you get the ball rolling? Tell us how the week went for you. We're all friends here."

More sideways smirks passed between Rochelle and Rachel, but I don't think Mr. Mac caught on.

Despite being a guidance counselor, Mr. Mac couldn't seem to understand or relate to older kids very well. He was the kind of person who liked to wear Disney ties, and he always carried his lunch around school in a Mickey Mouse lunch box—which all the little kids loved, of course. But his style definitely didn't work with sixth graders.

"Okay . . ." I tried to come up with something entertaining to say about recess. I knew I needed to work on this skill—being less serious and more jokey.

"It was crazy how many bloody noses there were," I said finally.

Which was true. There had been at least one or two at every recess.

"I swear it was like the kids literally rammed their faces into each other on purpose. Like . . . I don't know . . . a fourth-grade zombie apocalypse or something."

Surprisingly, the whole group cracked up at my lame joke. Rochelle spit out her popcorn, laughing and coughing, and Rachel had to pound her on the back. Even Veena covered a smile with her hand.

I felt this warm rush of pride. Maybe there was hope for me yet.

"Oh my gosh," Rochelle gasped when she could talk

again. "We had the exact same thing during the third-grade recesses, and we couldn't remember what to do. You lean forward to stop them, right?"

"No, backward, idiot"—Rachel smacked her arm.

Suddenly, Veena spoke up from the end of the table—a slight, whispery voice from a slight, whispery person. "Actually, I would like to say that for a nosebleed, it is best to sit up and lean forward slightly. Then you pinch your nose together lightly until the bleeding stops."

The two Rs gawked at her, and I felt like standing up and cheering for Another Smart Person. At the same time, I wanted to warn her to be careful. Speaking up could be dangerous. Especially when she got to sixth grade. *To speak or not to speak.* That was always the dilemma.

"My mother is studying medicine," the girl added softly, and hid behind her glasses again.

"Excellent." Mr. Mac clapped. "Thank you, Veena. Outstanding. So what else is going on out there at recess?"

Again the group fell silent. You could hear Mr. Ulysses, our school janitor, mowing outside. And the waspish buzzing of the fluorescent lights overhead. And some teacher (probably the gym teacher) yelling in the distance.

I wasn't sure why dead silence always made me feel so guilty, especially in class, but it did. Why did I think it was my job to say something when other people weren't saying anything? *To speak or not to speak.*

"Well, actually, I do have a question I wanted to ask," I said.

Mr. Mac gave a relieved smile. "Okay, great. What's your question, April?"

Since the bloody-nose comment had turned out okay, I decided maybe it was safe to bring up the more serious problem from my assigned recess: Joey Byrd.

After observing the fourth grader all week, I had no idea what to do about him. He acted so bizarrely, I thought something had to be wrong with him. Although I didn't know exactly what it was, I had some possible theories.

At home, I'd researched a little bit about autism, and I thought it was possible Joey Byrd might be autistic. He definitely had some of the characteristics: someone who wasn't very social (he never played with anyone at recess), someone who did repetitive things (the tree circles), someone who didn't make eye contact (lying on the ground with his eyes closed).

There was a boy in sixth grade named Wally Rensbacher who had a type of autism called Asperger's syndrome, so that's why I was sort of familiar with it. Wally's mind was like a presidential encyclopedia. If a president came up in any lesson, he would immediately raise his hand and begin reciting a bunch of facts about that president. Sometimes the teachers had to send him out of the room so they could keep teaching.

Although the other kids often avoided him, I didn't mind Wally. We'd actually worked on a research project together back in third grade. The teacher had assigned us to do a report on the moon (which, yes, morphed into a report on *President* Kennedy, who had a big impact on the moon landing program). Overall, it went pretty well.

Still, I felt uneasy bringing up my theory about Joey in front of the group. I wasn't an expert. Plus, I realized that whatever I said about him would definitely get passed around the school later on, courtesy of Rochelle and Rachel. And I wasn't sure if it was wrong to imply that someone might be autistic if they weren't.

I couldn't just ignore the problem, though. Maybe that was the Advice Box side of me. The side that always had to find the answers, even if they created more problems.

"Okay, so my question is about Joey Byrd, who's in my fourth-grade recess," I said carefully. "I was just wondering if, well, maybe he might be something like autistic?"

Notice I said *something like*—not that he *was* autistic.

"Autistic?" Mr. Mac leaned forward on his elbows, appearing confused by my question. "Why do you say that?"

Before I could answer, Rochelle jumped in with a sarcastic snort. "Because pretty much everybody knows that kid is abnormal."

"Autistic," I repeated, turning to glare at Rochelle. "I didn't say abnormal."

"Oh, okay." Rochelle rolled her eyes, and the table shifted as she kicked Rachel underneath it. Veena seemed to have turned herself into a block of stone.

"Let's stop the name-calling and allow April to finish talking," Mr. Mac warned.

Now I totally regretted opening my mouth to say

anything. I knew I needed to find a way to get out of the conversation—or change the subject, which was probably impossible by that point.

"I just didn't know if I should try to talk to him, or help him make friends at recess, or what," I stammered. "Right now it seems like everybody ignores him, and he, um, spent most of Wednesday's recess just lying on the ground with his arms out—"

Of course, this brought another sarcastic snort from the two Rs.

Mr. Mac shot a glare at them before saying, "Maybe he was just looking up at the clouds."

"Maybe," I replied slowly. "But his eyes were closed, so he couldn't really see them."

The counselor reclined in his chair. "Do you think it's possible he might have been daydreaming?" He tented his fingers under his chin. "You know, I remember being somewhat of a daydreamer like Joey when I was a kid. And people didn't always understand me either."

I tried to picture Mr. Mac as a daydreaming kid. Actually, you could kind of see it with his cartoon ties and the way he didn't seem to catch on to some things at first.

The counselor leaned forward. "But here's the irony: Daydreamers are the ones who often notice the things that nobody else does. They may seem like they're not paying attention, but then they end up being geniuses like Albert Einstein or Thomas Edison when they grow up."

A mocking eye roll passed between the two Rs. I

couldn't tell if Mr. Mac was saying Joey was a daydreamer, or a genius, or if he was avoiding my question altogether.

"So, um, you're saying he's *not* autistic," I repeated.

The counselor frowned a little. "Does it matter?"

The table moved again. I could tell Rochelle and Rachel were enjoying my public humiliation. My face got warmer. "I guess not."

"Good." Smiling, Mr. Mac crumpled the empty popcorn bag and tossed it toward the garbage can. He missed. He got up, retrieved it, and tried from just a step or two away. He missed again. Sighing, he dropped the crumpled bag into the can from directly above.

It landed in the right place this time.

"The point is—every child at Marshallville needs to feel like they are a valued member of the Tiger community," Mr. Mac said as he sat down again.

You could almost hear the silent groan from those of us who were sixth graders. We knew what was coming next. We'd heard this same speech since we were in kindergarten. *We Are All Tigers.* It was painted above the entranceway of our school. In large tiger-striped letters.

The counselor continued, "And it is our job as Buddy Bench leaders—as school leaders—to be *role models.*" His gaze focused sharply on the two Rs, and I held back a smile. "We need to show the younger kids how to get along with each other and *accept* each other's talents and differences. We need to show them we are all Tigers, right?"

Everybody nodded politely.

21

"So, April"—the counselor turned his attention to me again—"maybe you could try asking the other fourth graders to include Joey in their games, or you could engage Joey in conversation when he is by himself."

"Seriously? He actually *talks*?" This time it was Rachel whispering to Rochelle.

Rochelle hit Rachel's arm and snort-laughed. "Gosh, you are so *rude*. . . ."

How could anyone possibly consider them good role models for younger kids? I wondered. Was Mr. Mac hoping the Buddy Bench would magically transform them into nice people somehow?

Pretending not to hear the side comments (or maybe he didn't), Mr. Mac turned toward Veena and changed the subject. "So—what do you think? How do you feel about sharing a recess with one of the big sixth graders here to learn the ropes?"

Veena looked as if she had suddenly swallowed an egg. Whole.

"Share?" she repeated, carefully avoiding the gaze of the two Rs. It was clear she disliked them as much as I did.

"I was thinking perhaps you could partner with April since you both have the same lunch period," Mr. Mac added, smiling and pointing at me. (There were two fifth grade classes who ate lunch at the same time we did, so I figured she was in one of those groups.)

A wave of relief crossed Veena's face.

"Would that be okay with you, April?" the counselor asked.

I shrugged. "Sure. That's fine."

But I'll admit that I was a little annoyed by the idea. I'd applied for the Buddy Bench job so I could be alone, so I wouldn't *have* to be social. I didn't want to be in charge of entertaining a fifth grader every recess. I'd actually hoped to read a book or work on my writing when things weren't busy.

Mr. Mac stood up. "Excellent. Good meeting, everybody. That's all for today, ladies. See you next Friday." He herded our group toward the door.

As we left, I had to hold back a sigh. Nothing had really been accomplished in the meeting—well, except for assigning me a helper I didn't need.

I tried to tell myself that if the guidance counselor wasn't worried about Joey, maybe I shouldn't be either. No one else seemed to be wondering: Why does the kid walk in circles? Why does he lie down in the middle of things? Why does he spend all recess alone?

Maybe I was overthinking everything—which, I'll admit, I have a bad habit of doing. I knew I should focus on something else. Writing. Or school stuff. Or learning Mandarin Chinese (just kidding). Or whatever.

But ignoring Joey would turn out to be impossible.

On Monday, he brought the entire school to a standstill.

April: Fire Drill, Interrupted

Our principal, Ms. Getzhammer, was fanatical about fire drills. We had at least one a month (or so it seemed). She carried a thick pad of detentions to hand out to anyone who dared to talk, laugh, or even breathe during the drills. You could hear her steely voice echoing down the hall. "THIS IS SERIOUS, FOLKS. I BETTER SEE EVERYONE— AND I DO MEAN EVERYONE—TAKING THIS DRILL SERIOUSLY."

That's when Joey Byrd flopped down in the hallway and refused to move. Right in the middle of the orderly school evacuation drill. It was something no kid in their right mind would do. Maybe Joey did it back in third grade—the K–3 classrooms were in the opposite wing of the school—but I'd never seen it happen before.

I noticed the commotion as my class headed for our usual exit at the end of the hall. Even from a distance, I recognized Joey. He resembled an exotic butterfly on the hallway floor. Pale mop of hair. Bright blue shirt.

The rest of his class stood silently against the lockers gawking like open-mouthed fish while his flipped-out substitute teacher waved his arms in the air and tried to figure out what to do next.

As my class stopped in its tracks, the whispered comments flew down the line: "That's it. We're all gonna burn. We're all gonna be trapped here. We're all gonna die in a blazing inferno. Ahhh. . . ."

"DO I HEAR TALKING?" Ms. Getzhammer's voice cut like a wedge through the fake-panicked hum around me. The sixth graders spun forward and quickly shut up.

"Okay. Let's get going," Ms. Getzhammer barked, waving at Tanner Torchman, who was at the front of our line, bouncing from one Nike-clad foot to the other. His dad was the high school basketball coach. His mom was a vice president at Kellogg's. He could lead the sixth grade over a cliff, and, trust me, we would all follow him.

After my class left, I wasn't sure what happened next to Joey. I didn't know whether or not the principal hauled him away herself, or if she left him lying in the middle of the floor. Or if he finally got up and wandered outside on his own.

When the all-clear bell sounded a few minutes later, the hall was empty.

Everybody was convinced Joey would get a suspension—or at the very least a detention—for what he did. Ms. Getzhammer had been a middle school vice principal before she came to our school, so she wasn't the kind of person who let people off the hook. A lot of sixth graders referred to her as the Hammer.

Because the principal was normally pretty strict, I was

25

shocked when Joey showed up for recess that afternoon, the same as always. I was leaning against the Buddy Bench, waiting for Veena to appear. (Later I found out that she'd been assigned to work with me on Wednesdays and Fridays only.) Suddenly, at the back of the fourth-grade crowd streaming through the playground doors, I spotted a blue flicker. Joey's shirt.

I couldn't believe it.

First he waited for everyone else to go ahead of him. Then he opened the right-hand door to the playground as if it weighed about a thousand pounds. Making just enough room to squeeze past—nothing extra—he slid his skinny body through the smallest sliver of space.

Once outside, he wandered half-heartedly across the playground like somebody who'd been abandoned on a desert island—head down, hair awry—with one loose shoelace trailing behind him. A weird gold disk (stopwatch? compass?) dangled from a piece of red yarn around his neck.

Was he sad? Upset? Angry? It was impossible to tell.

Mostly, he looked totally alone.

In spite of promising myself on Friday that I wouldn't get involved, I could feel my older (and more sympathetic) self wanting to reach out to Joey and make things better somehow. In fourth grade—before Julie and I became friends—I used to draw pictures of myself as an alien whenever the girls in my class left me out of things. Which was often. So I could relate to the feeling.

"Hey, Joey, you can come over and hang out with me

for a while, if you want to," I called out. I pointed to the open space on the Buddy Bench and did my best to sound cheerful and big sister–like, even though I wasn't actually a big sister to anyone. In reality, I had a seventeen-year-old brother named Luke who seemed to forget my existence these days.

The boy glanced up at the sound of his name and squinted blankly in my direction.

"I'm April, one of the Buddy Bench helpers," I added.

Joey looked suddenly nervous and shook his head. His whispery reply drifted toward me like the jangle of a distant wind chime. "Thanks, I'm okay."

Then he flapped his hand in the air, as if telling me to go away, and made a beeline for the swing sets in the far corner of the playground. When he reached them, he glanced anxiously over his shoulder a couple of times as if to make sure I wasn't following him.

Okay, so that went well.

I sighed.

Sitting down, I flipped open my notebook and attempted to work on a poem about summer. Actually, it was a poem about Lake Michigan and the beach house where we go on vacation every year. I'd called the poem "Turquoise Summer" because of the brilliant color of the water.

In between jotting down some new lines, I kept an eye on Joey because I had this gut feeling that he was going to bolt. He kept glancing in the direction of Mrs. Zeff, who was watching a soccer game on the sports fields. You could tell he was just waiting for the right moment to take off. And who could blame him, right?

To be honest, the idea of running away occasionally crossed my mind too. When the social stuff at school was really bugging me, I would imagine going to our beach house and staying there until I was eighteen. Or I'd picture myself moving to some really remote place (like Alaska) where I could start over as someone completely new.

In my alternate world, I'd skip junior high and be in high school already. I would hang out with this small group of smart but loyal friends. I'd wear casually cool clothes, and I wouldn't care what people thought. And I'd change my name to something more fun sounding, like Haley or Jess.

Jess Boxler. Didn't that sound better than April?

Of course, I would never run away in real life—unless sitting on a playground bench by yourself at recess counted as running away. . . .

Fortunately, Joey seemed to lose interest in escaping after a few minutes. Out of the corner of my eye, I saw him wander toward the small metal slide near the swings. He was doing his usual foot-dragging walk again. Once or twice, he checked the gold disk around his neck.

From what I could tell, he appeared to be making a bunch of large curves instead of his usual circles. Every so often he would stop, turn in place, and drag his foot around in a tighter semicircle. Then he would jump to a new spot. He repeated the same bizarre pattern over and over: walk in a curve for a while, then stop, make a tight turn, and jump.

Surprisingly, he covered a lot of ground this way—nearly the entire area in front of the swings and slide. While he was focused on his feet, a soccer ball from the sports fields rolled right past him. Weirdly, he didn't even bother to glance at it.

Then a helicopter clacked overhead.

Freezing in midstep, Joey stared upward, transfixed, until it disappeared from view. Why was he so interested in the helicopter? I wondered.

The more I studied Joey, the more things I noticed. I made a mental list of them: How he walked with his hands clenched and his thumbs pointing outward like a hitch-hiker. How his gray sweatpants were way too short and the elastic bunched above his ankles. How his mouth was pressed into such a tight line of concentration, it didn't even look like he had lips.

What was he concentrating on?

It occurred to me that maybe the steps were some kind of a dance routine—the turns and hops sort of reminded me of one. Was he copying something he'd seen on television? Or in a YouTube video?

As the recess bell rang and the fourth graders poured into the building, I waited for him to notice time was up. He didn't. I finally had to wave and shout, "Hey, Joey, time to go in!"

He drifted over at last. I'm not sure Mrs. Zeff even realized he was still outside. She'd already gone into the building.

"Hey, I liked your dance," I said when he got close enough. "That was really cool!"

Joey stared at me with a blank expression. "What?" His dark, walnut-brown eyes were distant and hazy, as if he was miles away. A wood chip was stuck in his hair.

I probably should have given up at that point, but I'm stubborn and I don't quit easily.

"Hey, I was just thinking that you'll have to show me how to do that cool dance of yours someday," I said. "I liked it. It was really cool." Why did I keep using the word *cool*? Why did my voice sound so fake-happy?

"I don't know what you mean—goodbye," Joey said in a rush and speed-walked into the building—leaving me behind in the dust.

JOEYBYRD

Behind Joey, the playground was covered with curling lines—and a bunch of fourth graders' footprints.

The footprints really annoyed Joey, but there was nothing he could do about them. Things on the playground were always temporary. He didn't cry or get mad about it anymore, like he used to. He knew his tracings only lasted until 12:57, when the recess bell rang and everybody trampled his hard work like a herd of elephants.

So what were the lines supposed to be?

Waves, of course.

He'd made more than he realized. Big waves of water curled in front of the swings and the metal slide. They rolled past the old jungle gym that nobody ever used. They gathered and swooped toward the back doors of the school in a roaring rush.

Joey was sure that if the people in the helicopter were looking down, they probably guessed exactly what he was doing. It wasn't that difficult. You just had to put two and two—or three and three—together.

School. Fire drill. Waves.

You couldn't have an imaginary fire without an imaginary way to put it out, right?

It made perfect sense to Joey, even if the Buddy Bench girl didn't get it at all.

April: Riding Home

Strangely, the subject of Joey came up again on my bus ride home on Monday—which wasn't usually a place of great revelations.

I got to the bus late on Monday (due to a jammed locker problem), so most of the good seats were already taken. Normally, I liked a window seat in the third or fourth row.

Our driver's name was Hank. He was probably about fifty and he always seemed to be in a bad mood. I was convinced that either he hated kids or he wished he was driving a race car instead of a school bus. Or both. When there was no traffic on the road (and no one to report him to the police), he would accelerate around curves and gun the bus down the street—which was why I never sat in the front row. I didn't want to die.

But you couldn't sit too far back, because that's where some seventh- and eighth-grade boys from the local private school always sat. They got picked up before us. Although they wore ties and looked like mini-adults—trust me, they weren't. They would throw literally anything over the seats at you while Hank was driving: empty

Gatorade bottles, balled-up gym socks, dirt clods from their cleats, you name it.

It was always a tricky choice—getting killed because of the bus driver's bad driving vs. being nailed in the head by random objects thrown from the back.

When I finally got to the bus, there was only one aisle seat left a few rows back. A younger girl was already sitting against the window. Sighing loudly, I slid into the open spot.

The girl's eyes glanced sideways. "Hi."

I pushed back some straggles of hair from my face. "Hi."

Next to her feet, the girl had a pink plaid backpack that appeared to be almost empty. It kind of made me wish for those days before sixth grade when we didn't get homework in every subject. My backpack was the size and weight of a concrete boulder now.

The girl kept chatting. "I know you from the playground. You're the Buddy Bench person for us, aren't you?"

I mumbled and nodded. "Yeah, the fourth-grade recess."

"I'm in fourth grade."

"That's good." I forced a smile, because I was supposed to be a role model, right?

The girl leaned closer and whispered, "Hey, did you see what Joey Byrd did today during the fire drill?"

Weirdly, I felt suddenly protective of Joey—as if I was

his big sister and it was my job to defend him. Although my older brother, Luke, was often a jerk these days, he used to stick up for me when we were younger.

"Yeah." I shrugged as if it was no big deal.

"He's in my class, you know."

I didn't want to seem too curious about this fact, but I was. I couldn't help casually asking, "So, what's he like in class?"

"Well"—the girl sniffed—"everybody says he shouldn't be in fourth grade with the rest of us because he can't read or do math like we can. He has to go to tutoring for special help almost every day. And he gets into trouble a lot for not doing his work. My friends and I are reading books for *seventh* graders, you know."

"That's good," I answered automatically. But something else about Joey suddenly popped into my head.

I remembered how he'd left a couple of drawings in my Advice Box the year before. I hadn't paid much attention to them. Other than Joey's name, which was always written as JOEYBYRD, the notes had no words on them. They were just a bunch of scribbles and spirals drawn on torn pieces of construction paper.

I'd assumed Joey was just goofing around—or that he didn't understand what the box was for. The younger kids didn't always get the concept of advice, and Joey had been a third grader last year.

But now I wondered if I was wrong. Was it possible that he'd left the scribbles for me because he didn't know how to ask for help? Or because he couldn't read or write that well?

Gosh—I'd never even *considered* that possibility.

The girl next to me continued chattering. "Oh, and the other thing is he won't wear orange and black on Spirit Days, like everybody else. He didn't last year either," she added.

This might sound like a minor deal, but it wasn't.

We Are All Tigers wasn't just written above the doorway of our school—it was everywhere. School spirit was more important than just about anything in Marshallville, including cereal—which is saying a lot. Practically the entire city dressed in Tigers colors on high school game days.

"Maybe Joey doesn't own anything orange or black."

The fourth grader rolled her eyes.

"Or maybe his mom forgot to do the laundry—which has actually happened to me before," I added. "Or maybe his family is too poor to afford the latest spirit wear."

Nothing seemed to make an impact on the girl.

"Well, all the boys in my class hate him because he's a traitor and he doesn't like any sports," she continued. "And nobody will sit with him at lunch because he eats funny."

"Please." Sighing, I shook my head.

The girl's chin jutted out. "He does. He takes apart everything in his lunch."

"Takes apart?"

"He says, 'I don't like anything I can't see,'" she mimicked. "So he always pulls apart his sandwiches and puts

one piece of bread here and one here"—the girl panto-
mimed with her hands. "Then he takes out everything inside, like the meat and the lettuce and the cheese, and he
lays it all out on the table in front of him."

The girl wrinkled her nose. "It is *so* disgusting," she
said. "Then he usually eats the bread by itself like this."
She nibbled like a rabbit. "Then he eats everything else,
piece by piece, really slowly." The nibbling slowed.

"Unless it's pizza day." She paused in her mocking
demonstration. "Then he absolutely loves it and gobbles
up one or two slices in, like, five seconds." She gobbled up
an invisible pizza slice.

I didn't want to keep encouraging the girl, so I said,
"Okay, I get the picture. Thanks." I pretended to rummage
through the front zippered pocket of my backpack as if I
was searching for something. I hoped the girl would get the
clue that our talk was over.

"I'm not lying," she insisted. "You can ask anybody in
fourth grade."

"Okay."

"This is my stop." She lifted her almost-empty backpack and hugged it against her chest.

I was relieved to let the girl out of the seat. Clearly, a
pink plaid backpack didn't automatically make you a sweet
person.

After the fourth grader left, I kept thinking about Joey.
I jotted down a couple of the strangest details from the
conversation on the palm of my hand so I wouldn't forget

them (and because I was too lazy to look for a piece of paper).

I wrote: No Tigers stuff. Likes pizza. Can't read or write?

Then a watermelon Jolly Rancher suddenly ricocheted off the top of my head and onto the bus floor.

Wonderful. The barrage from the back was starting.

I slouched lower and tried to stay out of the line of fire for the rest of the ride.

April: Cattail Pancakes

Of course, my mom guessed right away that I had a new project. She took one look at my ink-covered palm while we were making dinner and said half-jokingly, "What? Did your school run out of paper again today?"

"I didn't want to forget something."

Smiling and shaking her head, my mom stirred a pan of taco rice on the stove.

I knew I was often a mystery to my mom. Not in a bad way—we were just polar opposites of each other in a lot of ways. I'd inherited her eye color (hazel brown) and her habit of being obsessively organized, but that was about it.

When she was in school, my mom was into sports much more than academics. She played varsity volleyball and ran track. Unlike me, she also had tons of friends—most of whom she still kept in touch with on Facebook. She was kind of a Facebook addict.

She also had a tattoo on the inside of her wrist—so it was pretty impossible to miss. It was a row of Chinese characters in blurry green ink. She got it when she went on a road trip out west with some of her girlfriends in college. "We were just being crazy," she said. "I think it says Peace and Harmony. At least that's what the tattoo guy told me."

I knew a lot of people had tattoos these days, so it was no big deal, but for some reason it embarrassed me—especially since my mom didn't know what it said. She was a physical therapist in town, and I always wondered if her patients noticed it and thought it was strange.

Julie Vanderbrook used to bring up my mom's tattoo a lot. I think she knew it bugged me. Once she brought it up at a sleepover and everybody (except me) ended up drawing fake characters on their arms for fun.

My dad had no tattoos.

He was a systems analyst for Kellogg's—which was data and spreadsheets basically. But he loved sports as much as my mom. He coached a Little League team in town called the Little Growlers. Although he was busy with work and coaching on the weekends, we always played chess together on Sunday nights after dinner. We called it our D&D Time (Dad and Daughter Time), and it was one of my favorite parts of the week. Sometimes my mom "advised" one of our sides, depending on who was winning or losing.

Probably the biggest disappointment to my parents was the fact that my brother and I had zero interest in anything athletic. Luke played music 24/7. He'd taught himself to play keyboard, drums, and guitar.

I was interested in just about everything else: Weather forecasting. Egyptian pyramids. Mammoths. The migration routes of whales. The Lost City of Atlantis. The *Titanic* disaster. Silent movies. Autism in fourth graders. You name it—I would literally read everything I could find on a topic until I was a mini-expert in it.

I remember how I went through a phase in third grade where I was absolutely obsessed with studying the wild plants the Native Americans and the pioneers used for food and medicine. I kept a little notebook with drawings of the most common ones. I tried to spot them when we were walking around outside. And yes, I'll admit that I even made my family eat a wild plant once.

Actually, it wasn't that dangerous. Or wild.

My mom and I were coming back from the grocery store one afternoon when I spotted some cattails—which are among the top twenty edible wild plants—growing beside the road. I convinced my mom to go back later so we could collect some of the brown tops. They are called catkins. (I loved that name.)

Of course, things didn't go exactly as planned. The ground was like a swamp, and our shoes got totally soaked collecting the cattails. (Mine were nearly sucked into the mud.)

Then we brought the catkins home and tried to collect the pollen by shaking them into a plastic bag. Supposedly, you could mix the pollen with pancake batter to make—yes—cattail pancakes.

I don't know what we did wrong, but all we got was a little yellow-brown fluff. (Maybe the catkins weren't quite ready.) We mixed it into the pancakes anyway.

My brother refused to try them, no matter what. He made us promise he could have the house if we died of cattail fuzz poisoning.

I didn't die.

Neither did my parents.

The point is I could be insanely determined about certain things until I found what I was looking for—even if it meant reading fifty books or eating cattail pancakes. And I think this explains why I was so determined to find the answers about Joey.

Today, my mom wasn't really into listening, though.

As I scrubbed my hands at the sink—whatever pen I'd used must have been semi-permanent—I tried to tell her about Joey. "He's part of my fourth-grade Buddy Bench recess," I explained. "And I think there's something definitely wrong with him, but nobody else seems to be worried about it."

Putting a lid on the pan of rice, my mom turned and glanced at me. Her lips were pressed together slightly. She didn't say anything, but I could tell she was wishing that I would spend my time on more normal sixth-grade problems.

For some reason, I kept going—as if I could convince her to be as interested in Joey as I was.

"Sometimes he walks around in circles outside. Like in spirals," I said, demonstrating with my hands. "And other times he lies faceup on the playground all recess with his eyes closed. Supposedly, he's having trouble in fourth grade—at least that's what I've heard—so I've been wondering if maybe he's autistic or something else like that. . . ."

At this point, I really wanted my mom to say how thoughtful—and mature—it was that I was interested in helping this kid. Or how wonderful it was that I'd noticed these significant things about Joey that nobody else had seen.

Instead, she said: "Wow. Sounds like a job for the professionals. Why don't you get Mr. Mac involved—that's the name of your guidance counselor, right? Let him know what's up with this boy. He definitely sounds like he needs some help—you're right."

Then she handed me a colander of washed lettuce to chop up for tacos. Annoyed by her advice, I dumped the lettuce on a cutting board and started chopping without saying another word.

My mom switched topics completely. "How about the kids in your class? Anyone you might want to have over this weekend? Maybe you could give Julie a call and do homework together? She hasn't been here in a while." Her voice rose hopefully.

Ergh. I wanted to press my hands over my ears. *Please don't start about friends.*

We had this same conversation about once a week.

No matter what I said, my mom never seemed to grasp the fact that girls today weren't the same as what she remembered from school. She didn't understand that being popular these days meant having long, swishy blond hair (with expensive salon highlights) and playing soccer (or some other team sport), and texting back and forth with your friends after your parents went to bed. None of which I did.

"No," I said in an irritated voice. "I'm fine."

"Okay," my mom replied quickly. "Just asking."

I knew my mom worried a lot about my lack of friends—and how it didn't seem to bother me. Back in the Julie Vanderbrook days, it wasn't all that different, even though my mom thought it was. Nine times out of ten, Julie was the one who called me to do something. Most of the time, I was perfectly happy sitting at home by myself reading about the life cycles of starfish or whatever.

I'm not saying I didn't want *any* friends. What I wanted were friends who wouldn't run off and get contacts and dye their hair pink and forget I existed. What I wanted were friends who would be there when you needed them . . . but you didn't need to hang out together all the time—or spend hours texting each other about meaningless stuff.

Did friends like that even exist?

After supper that night, I spent a couple of hours on the Internet. I searched random things like learning disabilities and autism and how to teach someone to read—I know this probably sounds excessive, but it was interesting. . . .

Of course, while I was trying to concentrate, my brother kept tapping his drumsticks on something in his room. It sounded like a deranged woodpecker on the other side of the wall. When I couldn't take it anymore, I went out into the hall, pounded on his door, and told him to shut up.

This time, Luke opened the door (which normally he doesn't do). In a half-awake voice, he said, "What? What's the big deal?" He had a bag of Doritos in one hand and two drumsticks in the other.

"I'm reading for school," I shouted back.

Tucking the bag under one arm, he leaned against the doorway, munching on a Dorito triangle. His fingertips were orange. It always surprised me how tall he was these days. And how he had this weird mustache of pale fuzz above his upper lip. "Reading what?" he asked. *"War and Peace? Canterbury Tales?* Shakespeare?"

I glared. "I'm reading about how to teach someone to read."

"What?" He squinted blankly at me.

"I'm reading about How. You. Teach. Someone. To. Read," I repeated slowly.

"Oh, that's easy." He grinned, licking the orange off his fingers one by one. "Ask me. I was the one who taught you how to read."

I rolled my eyes. "Right."

"Seriously, I did." Luke crossed his arms. "I was babysitting you one afternoon after school, and I opened up that Dr. Seuss book about fish. *One Fish Blue Fish* or whatever." He shrugged. "And I started pointing to each word, making you repeat it after me, and by the time Mom and Dad got home, you could read. I'm telling you, I was a freaking genius at teaching—"

"If you want to think that"—I squinted at him—"okay."

"Seriously, you should thank me for how smart you are. See, that big brain of yours—it's all because of me." He tried tapping one of his drumsticks on the top of my head, but I swatted his arm out of the way. Doritos scattered across the carpet.

"Great move," my brother said, swearing.

Although I helped him to pick up the Doritos, it didn't matter. Our brief brother-sister bonding moment was over.

Was my brother's story true or not? I had no idea. (Luke tended to exaggerate his own importance in everything these days.) I did have some hazy memories of the two of us reading books together on long car trips, but I didn't remember anything about my first book. Words just seemed as if they had always been there, surrounding me from birth. Like oxygen.

Which made me wonder how Joey could survive without them.

April: Reading, Continued

On Tuesday, Joey left another drawing in my Advice Box.

I always checked the box on Tuesday and Thursday mornings. This time, there were only two questions—and one wasn't really a question. It just said: "My teacher gives too much homework" with five exclamation points after it.

The other note was from a girl who wanted to know how to get invited to another girl's birthday party. The usual stuff.

Then, at the bottom, I spotted another spiral by Joey. This one resembled an exploding solar system. It was scribbled on a crumpled piece of black paper with silver crayon. Joey's name was squeezed into one corner: JOEYBYRD. All caps. No spaces.

As usual, I had no clue what the drawing was supposed to mean.

Later that morning, I was coming back from dropping off some stuff in the computer lab when I spotted Joey in the hallway. He was sitting at a desk, which I assumed someone (his teacher? a substitute?) had dragged out of the classroom.

His head was down on top of the desk, and there was a chapter book and some wads of notebook paper on the floor near his feet. I thought about asking him about the spiral, but I couldn't tell if he was already having a problem or a meltdown or what.

"Hey, Joey," I kind of whispered as I walked by, since the classroom door was open.

The fourth grader raised his head warily. His forehead was all blotchy, which could have been from crying or from having his face pressed against his arms. Or both.

"Hey, is that your book?" I pointed toward the floor with what I thought was an encouraging smile. I'm not sure why I brought up the book, since I already knew reading wasn't Joey's strength. Did I think he'd suddenly confess he couldn't read? Or ask me for help?

Of course, he didn't.

"Yes," he said in a flat, annoyed voice. "It is."

For some reason, I kept going. "So do you like the story? Is it any good?"

There was a smiling golden retriever on the jacket. The title was *Rescue!* I thought the story looked kind of appealing. If you were a fourth grader, that is.

Joey shook his head slightly.

"Well, the cover looks really fun with the dog and everything."

"No," he replied loudly. He folded his arms and flopped his head down on the desk again. "It isn't."

And that was as far as I got.

JOEYBYRD

Joey hated reading.

From above, most words were confusing and danger-ous. They stretched across the page in endless rows of peaks and valleys. If you weren't careful, you could easily fall into the narrow canyon of a V or the sliding valley of a U and never get out.

Joey fell into these spaces a lot—which was why he didn't like them.

But the worst letters were T F E Z.

They looked *exactly the same* from above, so Joey always had to turn them around in his mind to figure out which one was which.

This was exhausting.

Joey's favorite letter of the alphabet was i because of the dot. From above, the dot reminded him of a smooth, round stepping-stone in a dangerous river. Often he could tiptoe across a word on those dots as long as a j wasn't hiding somewhere in the middle.

Joey knew other kids didn't see words like he did. Letters didn't pretend to be canyons or valleys or rocks in a river. They weren't three-dimensional things. They stayed flat on the page. Almost anybody could figure them out—even stupid kids like the enemy boys who were in small-group tutoring with him.

Joey had learned that hiding his problem was better than pointing it out—like, even if you think you have a booger in your nose, don't pick it in public if you can avoid it.

But sometimes, even with a lot of practice and concentration, he would still mess up in class. He'd forget to look at letters the way other kids did. Or he'd get confused and accidentally see an F instead of a T. Or E instead of Z. He'd say the completely wrong word.

Then there would be loud hoots of laughter. Ha ha ha ha ha.

To make it stop, he'd throw all the words and letters into a big heap on the floor. Then his teacher would get mad at him for not treating books with respect. Throwing things is not acceptable, she'd say, and she'd pull his desk into the hall for a time-out.

The hallway tiles of Marshallville Elementary were tan-colored with lots of brown speckles, like the eggs of the great black-backed gull. The colors kept predators from seeing the eggs on the sand and eating them.

Sometimes Joey wished he was the egg of a great black-backed gull.

April: Veena Arrives

Veena finally showed up to work with me on Wednesday.

I had just draped my coat over the Buddy Bench be-cause it was warmer outside than I expected. When I turned around again, she was standing behind me with a polka-dotted lunch bag.

"Hi," she said, looking nervous. Her yellow Buddy Bench shirt was so long, it looked like a dress on her. I held back a smile.

"Wow, you're here! Welcome to your first day!" I said extra-cheerfully to set the fifth grader at ease. I moved my coat to one side to make more room.

"Thanks." The girl's fingers rolled and unrolled the Velcro top of her lunch bag. She didn't move. "I'm glad to be here."

"Seriously, you don't have to stand the whole recess." I pointed at the bench. "You're allowed to sit down on this *really comfortable* piece of blue plastic too."

The girl sat down on the far end of the bench and put her lunch beside her. Then she took about five minutes to tuck the extra fabric of her shirt underneath her pretzel-thin legs. I felt like a giant next to her.

"I think the shirt might be a little big," she said.

"Just a little." I grinned. "But maybe you can use it as a blanket when it gets cold. Or—a tent."

Both of us laughed, and Veena finally seemed to relax a little.

Motioning toward the playground, I gave her a quick overview of the fourth-grade recess before things got too crazy. I pointed out the various soccer and kickball teams on the big field beyond the playground. And the Pokémon boys who hung out by the side of the school and often got into arguments about their cards. And the clingy bracelet-making girls who were sitting in the meager shade of the 2003 Tree nearby.

"They'll definitely come over and offer you a bracelet before the end of recess," I whispered. "I already have about fifteen of them."

Friendship bracelets were the current obsession in the fourth grade. I was surprised that Ms. Getzhammer hadn't outlawed them yet, but I had a feeling she eventually would. Most of the fourth-grade girls had, literally, *stacks* of them on their arms. They were made of plastic string and colored beads, and they were always coming apart in the hallways and scattering beads everywhere. The sixth-grade boys loved crushing them under their shoes when they spotted them.

I pointed out Joey last.

Today he seemed to be trudging around the outer edges of the playground. He wore a pair of army-green Crocs instead of sneakers. Every so often, he had to stop and dump the wood chips out of the holes as he dragged his feet through the dirt.

"He is the person you spoke about at the meeting, right? The one who you thought might be autistic, right?" Veena shaded her eyes to look in his direction. She had a precise, almost British way of speaking.

I nodded. "Yes."

"Why is he doing that, do you think?" she asked, still squinting at Joey.

"Seriously, I have no idea. I've tried talking to him and he won't really communicate—except for pretty much telling me to go away."

"He seems to be making a large circle."

"It could be." I shrugged. "But every recess he does something different."

The girl glanced upward. The sun glowed butter-yellow above us. "Perhaps he is pretending to make a big sun?"

"Maybe . . ."

Almost as if he sensed he was being watched, Joey suddenly stopped and began shuffling through the middle of the circle toward us. He passed right in front of our bench, ignoring us completely, and kept going in a straight line to the opposite side of the playground, making a groove in the wood chips.

"Apparently *not* the sun," I joked.

"No," Veena said, still watching him curiously. "I guess not."

Joey crisscrossed back and forth a couple more times, making more grooves through the middle of his big circle. Then he started doing these odd jumping moves—jumping to an open spot and turning around in a small circle. He repeated the same movement again and again. Jump, spin. Jump, spin.

It was hard not to laugh. As Joey hopped from place to place with his face scrunched together and his hands clenched, he reminded me of an obsessed rabbit. I was amazed that nobody else on the playground had noticed what he was doing.

Veena asked me if I thought it could be a dance—which had been one of my first theories.

I shook my head. "No idea."

"Forgive me," the girl apologized, as if she was worried that she was getting on my nerves. "I ask too many questions."

Veena began to unpack her lunch, and I was surprised when she took out a bag of carrots and an ordinary peanut butter sandwich on white bread. Maybe I expected something more unusual because she was from India—which wasn't really fair, I guess. She could eat whatever she wanted.

I started unpacking my own lunch and tried turning the conversation in a different direction. "So, Mr. Mac said you moved here from India this summer, right?"

"Two summers ago," the fifth grader said. "We came to Detroit first. Then we moved here in July."

"So, um, why did your parents choose Marshallville, of all places?"

There were some kids from other countries in our school, but not many. There was a new boy from South Korea in sixth grade and two girls from Romania who had come in fourth grade. I think Veena was the only person from India, though.

Of course, I should have guessed the answer before she said it. Cereal.

"My father was hired by Kellogg's," the girl replied matter-of-factly.

"Oh—mine works there too." I grinned. "So which department is your dad in?"

"Product marketing. Bringing breakfast cereal to the world," Veena said in a singsong voice.

I laughed. For a fifth grader, she was pretty entertaining. And she was a lot more talkative than she'd been at the first Buddy Bench meeting.

"So . . . what are the biggest differences between living here and in India?" I asked, just because I was curious.

Veena quickly covered a laugh. "Smiling."

"Smiling?"

"Yes." She nodded. "At first I did not understand why everyone here in America smiled all the time. Or how big they smiled. All those teeth." She pointed to her tiny teeth. "Why was everyone smiling at me when they didn't know me and I didn't know them?" she said, shaking her head. "It made me quite nervous at first."

"Really?"

"Yes," Veena nodded solemnly.

"What else?" I asked.

"Well," she added hesitantly, "I was also surprised by how alike everything looked here."

"Alike?"

"The same colors," she explained. "In India, things are painted much brighter than here."

I laughed. "That's just Marshallville. We're boring."

"No no no," Veena rushed to say. "Just different."

But it was true. Our town was kind of like cereal.

I'm not saying Marshallville *literally* looked like a bowl of Corn Flakes, but most of the houses had been built around the same time, so they had a similar appearance. Picture a lot of two-story houses with beige or white siding, and large front yards, and one or two trees. That was Marshallville.

Most of our small downtown was the same style. Nothing was too colorful or noticeable.

Even the dogs you'd see around town were usually beige. (Golden retrievers were very popular.)

I wanted to ask Veena a few more things about India, but then chaos erupted around us. A couple of boys got into an argument over their Pokémon cards, and a kid with a bloody nose came limping from the soccer field.

Veena said she would take the bloody-nose kid to the nurse. I spent about fifteen minutes trying to convince the three Pokémon boys to calm down and give their cards back to the right owners. And then the recess bell finally rang.

After making one more jump and spin, Joey followed the other kids inside. He was the last one to leave the playground.

It was a crazy recess, but good.

JOEYBYRD

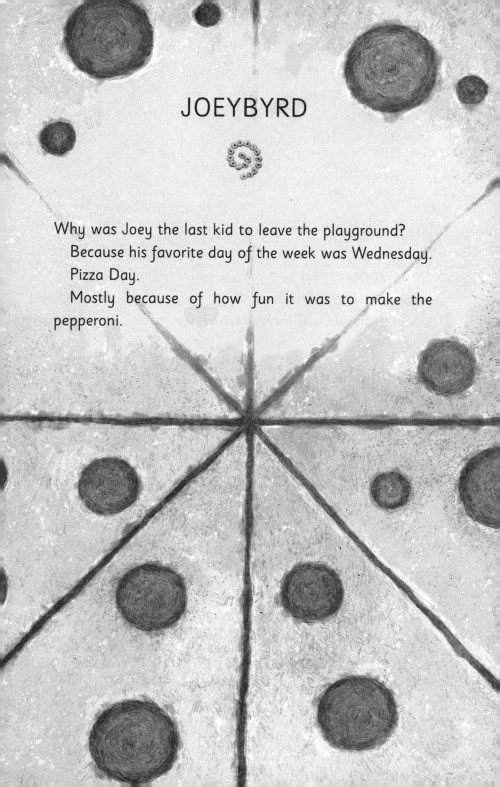

Why was Joey the last kid to leave the playground?
   Because his favorite day of the week was Wednesday.
   Pizza Day.
   Mostly because of how fun it was to make the pepperoni.

April: A Cheeseburger Mosaic

Things went downhill fast on Thursday.

I woke up feeling like I hadn't slept at all. I had one of those upsetting dreams where you are lost and wandering around empty buildings trying to find people who keep disappearing. I think I might have been lost in India at one point, because everything was painted in neon colors, and I kept smiling at everyone, and people kept running away from me.

Then my mom's alarm didn't go off, so she was late getting up for work. I didn't realize she'd overslept until she came rushing downstairs while I was getting breakfast.

"My alarm never rang. I don't know what happened. It just didn't go off," she said in a panic. "My hair is a complete mess, and I don't even have time to take a shower now." She ran her fingers through her short, scrunchy hair in a desperate attempt to make it look better—which only made it look worse.

Like I said, my mom is the kind of person who hates to be disorganized or unprepared. We were definitely alike in that way. As she smeared a giant glob of cream cheese on an untoasted bagel and frantically searched for her keys in her purse (they weren't there), I could tell she was getting more and more upset.

Then our cat, Sam, threw up his breakfast on our white living room carpet.

I was trying to help clean up that mess and look for my mom's lost keys when the school bus revved past our house, rattling the windows.

Add "missing the bus" to the list of morning catastrophes.

When we couldn't find the keys (we found out later that they had fallen between the sofa cushions), my mom finally had to call my dad to come back home and pick up both of us. By then she was crying. I ended up being a half hour late to school and missed a quiz. And I forgot to bring my lunch, so I had to ask for permission to leave my language arts class early to buy one before my Buddy Bench time started. Luckily, my teacher didn't care and let me go.

Of course, it was cheeseburger-and-fries day—one of my least favorite days to buy. The fourth graders were still eating in the cafeteria when I got there.

As I stood in line, I noticed Joey sitting nearby. You couldn't really miss him—first, because he sat at one of the tables next to the line. Second, because his lunch didn't look like anyone else's. It was spread across the table in front of him, just the way the girl on the bus had described it.

It looked like a food mosaic. One hamburger patty and two bun halves were arranged in a row on a brown paper napkin like this: bun, patty, bun. Six crinkle fries had been lined up below them. A carton of chocolate milk sat on one side of the napkin, and Joey's cafeteria tray was on the opposite side. In each of the tray's dividers, Joey had placed a different food item as if they were a museum display: a leaf of wilty lettuce, an onion circle, a pickle slice, and a paper cup of ketchup.

What I wish I hadn't seen was what happened next.

As I stood there, one of the boys sitting a few feet away from Joey—a tank-sized kid with a buzz cut—suddenly slid toward him and smacked the corner of Joey's tray with his fist. Hard.

Instantly, everything went flying.

Joey's pants got hit with blobs of ketchup. The pickle and onion landed on the floor near his feet. The fries scattered across the bench. His tray landed upside down on the floor. The tank-sized kid started laughing and pointing out the mess. Pretty soon the whole table was a riot of laughter.

Of course, I couldn't let that go.

"Save my spot," I said to one of the fourth graders behind me. "I'll be right back."

Walking over, I waved my arms and yelled at the tank kid. "Hey! What do you think you're doing? Why did you mess up his lunch?" The rest of the kids at the table stopped laughing and stared at me.

"Whaaaat?" The tank kid's voice was shrill.

"You dumped that other kid's lunch all over the floor." I waved an arm vaguely toward Joey and pretended not to know his name.

"No, he did it himself. Didn't you, idiot?" The kid's hand smacked Joey's arm. Hard.

Joey stayed frozen in place, staring vacantly at the air molecules.

"No, I was standing right over there." I gestured at the cafeteria line. The line kids were all staring now. "I saw you reach over and hit his lunch. So you get up and get him a new one. Now."

I was surprised at how adult (and official) I sounded. Like I was channeling Ms. Getzhammer herself. Furiously, I jabbed one finger in the direction of the lunch line. "Seriously, go and get him a new lunch like I said. Tell the lunch ladies you ruined Joey's lunch and he needs another one."

"What?" The stupid kid's voice shrieked higher. "But they'll make me pay for it and it isn't my lunch. I didn't do it."

"I said Get. A. New. Tray. For. Him. Or I'll go and find Mrs. Zeff and tell her what you did."

I was pretty sure steam was coming out of my ears at this point. Usually I wasn't the kind of person who would yell at anyone (even fourth graders). But seeing a defense-less kid get picked on—it made my whole body feel as if it had been set on fire.

The boy slammed backward. "Stupid moron!" He swore at Joey as he barreled toward the lunch line. The kids at the table started whispering and eyeballing me to see my reaction.

Smiling at Joey, I shook my head to communicate that

I was on his side, that the other kid was completely out of line, but Joey's face stayed blank and expressionless. I couldn't tell if he was happy I'd helped him or upset by the tank kid's words or anything. It looked as if he'd disappeared from his own body.

"Keep your hands to yourselves and don't touch anyone else's lunch," I warned the group in my new voice of authority.

Fortunately, Mrs. Zeff and another teacher arrived after that. They supervised the cleanup and made sure the tank kid returned with a decent lunch for Joey—which he did.

I figured maybe Joey would thank me later on, when he came outside for recess, but he didn't utter a word to me—or show any emotion at all. Not even a grateful smile or a nod. It kind of bugged me. Especially with how crappy the whole day had been—a little appreciation would have been nice, you know?

Joey did nothing except walk in a giant spiral for the entire recess. That's all.

One big spiral.

JOEYBYRD

Joey started his spiral with the first thing that went wrong that day—the enemies on the bus snapping his good pencil in half and laughing like hyenas; then he added the second thing, which was getting a zero in science for forgetting his homework, then the boy with the spiky hair smacking his lunch tray and sending everything flying, then the word "moron"—

The spiral got bigger.

"Moron" made him think of other words—idiot, dork, loser, freak—and more things like getting his desk dragged into the hallway for not treating books with respect—and the substitute teacher yelling at him during the fire drill—

He kept walking.

The spiral got bigger.

Yelling made him think of the gym teacher, who was mad about his Crocs on Tuesday—and nobody being his partner in gym class—and his mom who didn't like the two Cs and one D and one F on his weekly progress report—and his dad who wouldn't build Legos with him if he didn't try harder this week—

He kept walking.

The spiral got bigger.

He walked until everything spiraled and circled around him—until his sadness spun around the skinny maple tree, and around the playground, and around the school, and around Marshallville, and around the cereal factories, and maybe even around the universe itself— pulling everything with it, before it finally disappeared like water going down a drain.

And then Joey felt better.

April: Spirit Day

Fortunately, Friday started out as a better day than Thursday. It was sunny when I woke up, and I could hear my mom making coffee downstairs, so I didn't need to worry about another alarm-clock disaster with her.

It was our third Spirit Day of the football season. As I pulled on my orange Tigers T-shirt, I felt more excited than I usually did. The shirts were brand-new. All week, the sixth graders had been buzzing about them. They had our school district's mascot—a tiger face—on the front. On the back, the shirts listed our class graduation year with all our names in tiny white print.

A lot of the sixth graders planned to wear them to the game that night.

Last year, I'd gone to only two football games—one with Julie and her parents, and another with my parents.

Of course, like everything else this year, things had changed. Going to the games had become a matter of *national importance* now. And you couldn't sit with your parents any longer. That was very uncool.

In sixth grade, you had to go to the football games with a group of friends. Which meant you actually needed to *have* friends. The bigger the group, the more popular you were. Trust me, the games and who-was-going-with-who were the *only* topics of conversation on Fridays.

Normally, I dreaded Spirit Days and tried to pretend I didn't care about any of it. But the new shirts made me feel a little more hopeful. At least they made us *look* like we were one big happy family even if it wasn't true. Plus, I didn't have to stress about what to wear, like I usually did during the week.

When I stepped outside in the morning, the sky was the turquoise color of Lake Michigan. A beautiful cloud puff drifted overhead like a hot-air balloon. I swear you could even smell the faintest scent of sugary Froot Loops in the air—which usually only happened in the summertime when it was warm and the wind was blowing in the right direction from the cereal factories.

I took a deep breath, feeling summery and hopeful.

At school, my first class of the day on Friday was gym class.

If it was a Spirit Day, Mr. Dunner, the gym teacher, usually gave all of us open gym—which meant you could do what you wanted. Read, study, play basketball, finish homework, or whatever.

I'd already planned to work on my next advice column. It was going to be about a girl who didn't want to be on a swim team anymore, even though her parents wanted her to stay. TELL ME HOW TO QUIT, PLEASE!!! she had written in all purple caps on her Advice Box note, so how could I ignore that, right?

But the minute I walked into the gymnasium on Friday morning, my perfect day came crashing down.

It was clear that we weren't going to get a free gym day. Mr. Dunner had obviously planned some kind of awful obstacle course or relay competition for us. Giant truck tires, balance beams, hurdles, orange traffic cones, and various other obstacles had been scattered around the gym. Worst of all, the climbing rope now dangled from the ceiling to the floor.

No way.

I had hoped to get through sixth grade without ever facing it again.

The rope had always been my nemesis. In third grade, I'd fallen flat on my face while attempting to climb it. Seriously. For some reason, I'd tried to make a running leap at the rope—maybe I thought the momentum would propel me upward—but I'd completely missed it and face-planted on the mats instead. The whole class had died laughing. Then I'd started crying, and the gym teacher had to call the school nurse to come and get me.

It was one of my most embarrassing school memories.

As Mr. Dunner started our class, I scrambled to come up with a good reason for being excused. Could I have a headache? Or a stomachache? Or say I felt like I was getting sick with the flu?

The gym teacher began dividing everyone into groups. I was only half listening. Mostly, I was completely panicking. I didn't realize I'd been placed in Tanner Torchman's group until Julie Vanderbrook smacked my arm and hissed, "No fair, you're in *his* group."

"Girls!" Mr. Dunner yelled, pointing directly at us. "I'm giving directions here."

I took a couple of steps back.

I was still panicking about how to get out of class as the gym teacher toured us around the gym, showing off the different stations. When he got back to the climbing rope, he pointed at the orange flags tied on the rope every three feet or so. "At this station, the team captain will record the height each person reaches," he said. "We'll add up the heights at the end to get a team total."

I knew I wouldn't make it to the first flag above my head.

"So do we have a volunteer to demonstrate this activity?" Mr. Dunner asked.

Of course, the class nominated Tanner Torchman. He was the undisputed king of everything athletic at Marshallville, including rope climbing. Nobody else came close. Nobody even tried to come close.

And of course I had to get placed in his group.

Shaking his head and smiling in this half-embarrassed way, Tanner stepped onto the mats. He ran his hands through his perfect swoosh of hair. Then he rubbed his palms on his gym shirt as if they were sweaty—which I'm sure they weren't—and took a deep breath. Everybody started chanting as he reached for the rope.

"Tan-ner! Tan-ner! Tan-ner!"

He began to climb. In just a minute or two, he had shimmied effortlessly all the way to the top of our gymnasium. I'll admit—it was kind of amazing to watch. After high-fiving one of the orange-painted beams, Tanner stayed there—at the top of the gym—surveying his kingdom like a golden-haired Tarzan.

"Hey, what can you see from up there?" someone yelled.

"The tops of everybody's heads," Tanner shouted back. "And Mr. Dunner's big bald one."

The gym teacher rubbed his shaved head and bellowed, "THAT'S IT. A BIG FAT F FOR YOU, TORCHMAN." The class laughed.

"Jacob," Tanner shouted to one of the popular kids in his group. "Dude, I swear it's like I can't even see you now. It's like you're invisible."

Jacob West was a skinny, freckle-faced kid who spent most of his time goofing around with Tanner in class. I think he must have owned every Michigan State jersey ever made. They were the only shirts he ever wore except for our Marshallville ones.

Just showing off, Jacob flopped down on the mats and stretched out his arms dramatically. "Hey, moron, can you see me now?" he yelled.

In that instant, something clicked in my mind. I pictured Joey lying faceup on the playground just like Jacob. Arms out. Eyes closed. I thought about how he'd stared, transfixed, at the helicopter that had passed overhead at recess one afternoon. I remembered the giant spirals he'd made in the wood chips with his feet.

As Tanner and Jacob continued shouting insults back and forth to each other, my eyes kept shifting between the two of them. Was it possible that Joey was looking at things the same way? I wondered. Was he picturing himself like Jacob on the ground? Or like Tanner above? Was he imagining things the way a helicopter would see them? Or like a bird flying over?

Oh! Another jolt of realization hit me. Joey Byrd—*Bird*.

I think I might have gasped out loud, because some of the kids who were standing nearby turned around to stare at me as if I'd just done something weird.

I was so caught up in thinking about this bizarre idea—Joey as a hypothetical bird—that I completely missed my chance to get out of class. By the time I realized what was happening, Tanner had come back down to earth and all the groups were moving to their stations. Of course, Tanner's group had to start with the rope.

"Okay, everybody on my team, get in line," he shouted, and waved his arms.

Standing at the very end of the line, I tried to tell myself I'd probably never get to the front. If I was lucky, we'd move to a different activity before my turn ever came up.

While everyone around me went crazy cheering and rooting for each other, I kept thinking about the possibility of a fourth grader who saw the world like a bird because his last name was Byrd. Was it a ridiculous idea? Could it explain why Joey acted the way he did? How could I figure out if I was right?

Suddenly, someone pushed me from behind. "April, you're next."

I looked around thinking there had to be some mistake. Everybody in my group couldn't have taken a turn already. The line couldn't have gone that fast.

But Tanner was waiting next to the mats with his clipboard. He nodded at me. "Okay, go ahead," he said.

I felt like passing out and throwing up at the same time.

"I don't want to do this," I heard my voice say out loud as I took one small step forward.

And that's when the unexpected happened.

Instead of laughing or making some smart comment, Tanner shrugged and said, "Okay, forget it. You can just get back in line and I'll make up something for you."

What? I wasn't sure I'd heard him right.

"Get back in line?" I repeated in this numb voice.

"Sure," Tanner said, scribbling something on his clipboard. "You're fine. I've got you covered, April."

Usually I didn't like the sound of my own name. Too weird. Too spring-ish. But when Tanner said it, my name actually sounded kind of normal and sweet—as if he said it all the time, as if we were good friends.

Of course, a couple of the stupid girls who were milling around nearby started complaining about me getting a break. "Hey, we had to take our turns," they whined, flicking their hair around. "Why didn't April have to do anything?"

Tanner shrugged. "Because Coach Dunner says I'm in

charge of this group. Sue me if you don't like it." He smiled and the girls laughed as if this was the funniest thing they'd ever heard.

I resisted rolling my eyes.

"Thanks," I whispered in Tanner's direction before I headed toward the back of the group again.

I had no clue why Tanner let me off the hook—maybe he remembered my climbing disaster of the past, maybe he was just being nice, or maybe he didn't want my pathetic score to ruin our team's chances of winning—but I went through the rest of gym class feeling like I was floating above everything.

April: Watched

For the rest of the morning, I barely paid attention to anything. We were doing algebraic equations in math—that's all I noticed. In language arts, we watched a movie. The rest of the time, I kept thinking about my new theories for Joey.

Was it possible that he was making something on the playground—like a picture, or a pattern, or a message—as he wandered around? Did you have to see it from above to understand what it was? And how could I do that?

(Okay, I'll admit that my mind replayed the scene of Tanner saving my life in gym class a few times, too.)

When lunchtime finally arrived, I was outside before Mrs. Zeff.

Joey was easy to spot in the sea of Tigers shirts pouring through the playground doors from the cafeteria. Everyone else was dressed in orange and black. He was the only one wearing red. Red T-shirt. Red jacket. Faded red soccer pants. Green Crocs.

As I watched Joey's meandering path across the playground, a fourth-grade girl tapped my arm. "Hi, April. Do you want to make friendship bracelets with us today?"

No, I didn't.

Two other girls stood beside her, looking hopeful with their plastic bags of beads and string. I glanced around for Veena. It was Friday, one of her assigned days to work. Where was she? I felt slightly annoyed that she was missing. What was the use of having a partner if she didn't show up?

"Sure, okay," I reluctantly agreed.

Taking a seat on the Buddy Bench, I tried to appear interested in whether to make a bracelet with "peace" or with "friendship" spelled out in beads while keeping an eye on Joey at the same time.

He seemed to be making a large wavy circle around the edges of the playground.

By the time Veena finally appeared, a whole crowd of fourth-grade girls were sprawled around the Buddy Bench. Sitting on the ground, they passed beads and colored string back and forth to each other.

"I'm sorry I'm late," Veena apologized in a rush. "We had a guest speaker today."

"No problem," I said.

As Veena sat down, I checked on Joey again. He had finished walking around the outside of the playground and he was working on two smaller circles nearby now.

"Hey, I think I'm going to go over and try to talk to Joey a little," I whispered to Veena. "Are you okay staying here for a few minutes without me?"

Veena nodded. Her eyes darted toward Joey. As we

watched, he pivoted like a soldier and dragged his foot in the dirt, making a short line near one of his circles. Veena half smiled and shook her head.

Of course, the girls around us overheard Joey's name and had to put in their two cents. "He's such a traitor," they said, making no attempt to hide their dislike of him. "Look. He's wearing red. He did it on purpose, you know, so we'll lose the game tonight. Red and white. That's the Spartans' colors."

I had no idea if this was true or not. I didn't even know for sure who our football team was playing. That's how much I cared about football.

Veena attempted to change the subject. "Okay, okay, back to the bracelets." Reaching into her pocket, she brought out a handful of beads that didn't look like the usual cheap plastic. They were brightly colored ceramic beads, with silver and gold ones mixed in.

The diversion worked. The girls lost interest in Joey, and I took off without being noticed.

The rest of the playground was mostly empty. There was a small group of boys sitting next to the slide, trading cards. Two girls talked on the swings, but everyone else was out on the sports fields.

"Hey, Joey," I called out as I approached. "What are you making today?"

He stopped in midstep.

"What?" He glanced toward me.

"I was just wondering what you're making on the playground today." I pointed at the cluster of lines he'd just finished nearby. "Is it supposed to be a picture or something?"

"No, it's my tracing." Joey's voice sounded annoyed.

"What do you mean by your tracing?" I wanted to keep the fourth grader talking. "Could you explain what you mean?"

Joey ducked his head down. "It's what I make. That's all."

Then he pivoted away from me and walked stubbornly in the opposite direction.

Sighing, I glanced toward our school's old jungle gym and considered whether or not to climb it. The rusty, beehive-shaped structure was pretty much my only option (other than the roof of the school) if I wanted to see anything useful. Although it was the tallest thing on the playground, it was so old that the little kids didn't even play on it anymore. I hadn't set foot on the thing in years.

As I strolled over to the metal structure, my biggest fear was that someone in the sixth grade (Tanner Torchman, for instance) would spot me from the cafeteria. The windows at the far end of the lunch room faced the playground. I knew if someone saw me, I'd never live it down. *Hey, did you know April Boxler actually plays on the old jungle gym at recess? Ha ha ha ha.*

Normally, the sixth graders wouldn't notice anything outside the cafeteria during lunch. They were too wrapped up in their own little worlds. But I was still afraid of being spotted by accident, so I knew I needed to be fast.

I stepped onto one of the lower metal bars. As I reached for the next one, a powder of orange rust came off on my palms.

Great.

Trying not to get completely covered in rust-orange, I skipped about half the rungs as I scrambled awkwardly upward. At the peak, I held on to the top bar with one hand and turned around carefully to survey the playground.

The view was disappointing.

I could see most of the lines Joey had made. In the middle of the playground, there were two perfect circles with a clump of diagonal lines near each one. A faint, wavy circle went around the perimeter of the playground. A lot of random squiggles seemed to go nowhere.

But the jungle gym wasn't high enough for me to figure out if the marks were part of any bigger plan or design. Plus, Joey had stopped working and was now lying in the middle of his lines—arms angled out slightly from his sides, eyes closed—pretending to be dead again. (As usual, I worried that maybe he was.)

Then the recess bell rang.

From my perch, I watched the stampede toward the doors. Soccer players, flag football teams, kickball kids, friendship-bracelet groups—all streamed toward the school like a migrating herd of orange and black. It was an interesting perspective to have. I felt both invisible and important, powerful and powerless, at the same time. Was this the way Joey saw the world? I wondered.

As the last couple of girls picked up their bracelet stuff and left, Veena kept glancing toward the jungle gym as if she wasn't sure what to do next. She took a few steps closer to Joey, and I think she must have told him that recess was over. He finally got up, shook the wood chips out of his hair, and ambled slowly inside.

By then, I was almost alone on the playground—nearly everyone else had disappeared inside except Veena and Mrs. Zeff, who was standing by the playground door impatiently.

I started to scramble down the metal rungs—there really was no graceful way to do it—when a slight movement on the roof of the school caught my eye.

Glancing upward, I was convinced I saw the shadow of a person duck down—or at least, it looked like someone was on the roof, and then they weren't.

My heart pounded. Why was someone hiding on our school roof? I wondered. Were they watching the playground? Or us?

It made me feel both curious and creeped out at the same time.

Who was watching our playground—and why?

April: The Secrets of Mr. Ulysses

Veena hadn't noticed anything unusual. When I asked her if she saw anyone on the roof at the end of recess, she said she didn't even look in that direction.

"I'm sorry. I was too busy helping the girls pick up all their beads. I should have been more observant," she apologized.

"No, no. That's okay," I reassured her. "I'm not even sure what I saw."

But the whole thing bothered me so much that I decided we should talk to Mr. Ulysses, the janitor, before we went back to class—just to let him know. He was the resident expert on almost anything at our school. He was also the easiest adult to find, since his office was closest to the playground and the cafeteria. I pointed out his door to Veena, once we got inside. It said Boiler Room on it.

"That's an office?" she said, looking doubtful.

"Yep. You'll see."

I knocked, and a distant voice boomed, "Hullo! It's open. Come on in!"

I pulled on the heavy door. Behind me, Veena took a quick step backward as a blast of pungent, steamy air poured out. Marshallville Elementary had been built before World War II. It was still heated with ancient water boilers and rattling steam pipes, but Mr. Ulysses didn't seem to mind the noise and the heat.

He sat in his usual spot—an old wooden desk in the far corner of the cluttered and badly lit room. He was a stout, grandfatherly man with a short gray beard and these cheerfully bright eyes that never seemed to look annoyed by anything. I wasn't sure how old he was, but he'd been at Marshallville for years.

"Hi, Mr. Ulysses," I said.

"April!" Smiling, the janitor got up from his sagging office chair and wiped his grease-stained hands on a rag. "You caught me fixing a motor from one of my pesky lawn mowers."

Mr. Ulysses was always working on something. His desk was a fascinating symphony of stuff—parts and pieces of things in need of repair—along with newspapers, junk mail, fast food wrappers, and drawings from kids. Above his desk, there were literally *layers* of kids' artwork and a homemade plaque with MR. ULYSSES spelled out in soda pop tabs.

I was probably the only student who knew the real story behind the janitor's unusual name.

Last year, he'd told me how his dad had been a high school teacher who loved Greek and Roman history. Apparently, Ulysses (also called Odysseus) was a legendary Greek king and hero, and so that's why his dad had named him Ulysses. Although it was actually his first name, he used it as a last name at school as a way to honor his dad, which I thought was really cool.

I had read more about Odysseus later on and I discovered that he was also known for his ingenuity and inventiveness. (He was the creator of the Trojan Horse.) I thought this was a pretty surprising coincidence since our Mr. Ulysses could also fix virtually any problem. The teachers were always calling him for help.

I swear Mr. Ulysses even *looked* like some of the illustrations I found of Odysseus: Short beard. Curly hair. Sloping nose. Was our janitor a Greek hero in disguise?

The idea always made me smile.

"Everything okay, April?" Mr. Ulysses squinted at me. "I haven't seen you around lately."

"I'm sorry. I've been really busy," I replied, feeling guilty that I hadn't stopped by the Boiler Room once to say hello. I silently vowed to make more of an effort.

"I wanted to introduce you to someone new. This is"— I pointed toward Veena.

"Wait, don't tell me," the janitor interrupted. He closed his eyes and pressed his fingers to his forehead. "New student. Fifth grade. Parveena . . ." He opened his eyes. "Am I right?"

In addition to being able to fix anything, he could recall the first name and grade level of every student in the school. All eight hundred of them.

Looking surprised, the fifth grader reached out her hand. "Yes, thank you. You can call me Veena. Nice to meet you."

"Veena." Mr. Ulysses smiled, shaking her hand. "Got it."

"We just have one quick question," I continued, trying to make it sound minor.

"Okay, go ahead." Mr. Ulysses sat down again.

"Well, Veena and I are both helping with the Buddy Bench this year," I said. "And it's probably no big deal— but I thought I might have seen someone on the roof today during the fourth-grade recess. It could have been a shadow, or my eyes, or something, but I thought we should stop by and mention it."

Turning around, Mr. Ulysses squinted at the clock hanging on the wall above his desk. "Well, as a matter of fact, I was on the roof today. About ten minutes ago."

I felt a rush of relief. "Oh, then it must have been you."

"But while I was up there today," Mr. Ulysses continued with a sly smile, "I just happened to notice that *you* were standing on top of the old jungle gym for some reason. And you seemed to be very interested in the work of our good friend Joey Byrd too."

Although Mr. Ulysses often noticed the little things that nobody else did—different haircuts, new glasses, lost lunches, jammed lockers—his words still took me by surprise.

"So you already know about Joey?"

The janitor chuckled. "Well, let's say I'm trying . . ."

Behind me, Veena spoke up. "We keep watching him. But we don't understand what he is doing at recess every day."

Mr. Ulysses thunked his work boots on top of the piles on his desk. "So let's hear it." Smiling, he gave us a curious look. "What's your best theory about him?"

Veena glanced uncertainly toward me.

In my head, I ran through all the different Joey possibilities: Autistic kid. Daydreamer. Aspiring YouTube dancer. Or (most bizarre of all) pretending to be a bird.

"I'm not sure," I replied cautiously. "It just seems like there's a purpose to what he's doing, but we haven't figured out what it is yet. . . ." My voice trailed away.

"Go on," Mr. Ulysses prompted. "Explain what you mean."

"Well, the most recent idea I had"—I started out hesitantly, unsure of how much to reveal—"I know it probably sounds crazy, but it came to me during gym class this morning. We were doing rope climbing and Tanner Torchman climbed to the top of the gym—"

"Isn't he unbelievable?" The janitor smiled and shook his head. "Mark my words—that kid is going to be a big football star someday."

"Well, seeing Tanner at the top of the gym gave me another idea," I continued. "I started thinking about how we look at things. For instance, maybe Joey doesn't see things the way we do. Maybe you have to look at what he's doing from above. You know . . . like a bird's-eye view." I gestured vaguely toward the pipe-filled ceiling of the boiler room. "So that's what I was trying to figure out today. If there was any pattern or design on the playground. . . ."

"Go on . . . ," Mr. Ulysses said, raising his eyebrows. "I'm with you."

"But I couldn't see anything, really." I shrugged and shook my head. "At least nothing that I recognized. It was all just random lines and circles. So now I'm totally out of ideas."

"Hmm . . ." Mr. Ulysses gazed at the ceiling as if he was thinking.

Standing up, he gestured toward a metal ladder in the far corner of the boiler room. It was attached to the back wall. I'll admit I'd never noticed the ladder before—or the square trapdoor above it, which had to lead to the roof, I guessed.

"Follow me," the janitor said mysteriously.

Despite his age—and a lot of years of eating birthday treats from kids—Mr. Ulysses ascended the narrow ladder quickly. At the top, he grunted as he turned a handle and pushed the trapdoor upward, sending a sudden blaze of sunlight into the gloomy room. After he crawled through the open space, he called down to us.

"Okay, come on up, April and Veena." His bearded face loomed large in the square above us. Maybe it was my imagination, but the sunlight behind him almost made it look as if he was wearing a crown. It made me think of the Greek hero Odysseus again.

"Your turn now. Be careful," Mr. Ulysses said.

Reaching for the sides of the metal ladder, I felt slightly more courageous than I'd been with the rope in gym class.

At the same time, I couldn't help worrying about how this was making us *really* late to class, and I knew I should probably tell Mr. Ulysses that we needed to leave. I didn't want to get Veena into any trouble.

But it turned out to be a pretty quick climb. Mr. Ulysses steadied my arm as I scrambled through the opening and emerged on the warm black-tar roof, feeling victorious. I gave Veena a hand behind me. Her tiny fingers felt like a bundle of sticks.

"Welcome to the top of the world," Mr. Ulysses said once we reached the rooftop.

The turquoise-blue September sky stretched overhead, dotted with the same cheery cloud puffs I'd seen earlier that morning. Although Marshallville Elementary was only a single-story building, except for the gym, it seemed much higher from our lofty viewpoint.

"Wow, this is so great." I walked around the rooftop a little, trying to take in everything—the sky, the drifting clouds, the views. I'm not crazy about heights, but the roof didn't seem to bother me.

Shading her eyes, Veena looked awed by it all. In one direction you could see the white globe of our city water tower, the stadium, and our high school. In another direction—the hazy shapes of the Kellogg's buildings and factories. They were actually in Battle Creek, but you could see them from Marshallville.

"Be careful where you step," Mr. Ulysses warned. Smiling, he pointed to a large splat of glistening white as we moved to the side of the roof that overlooked the playground. "Birds really like it up here."

I couldn't believe we were on the roof *during school*. It felt like winning an award for something—only I didn't have to feel guilty or embarrassed for winning because nobody knew about it.

"Okay, see what you notice on the playground now." The janitor rested one boot on the short ledge that surrounded the roof and gestured at the scene below us. All the recesses were over, so the Buddy Bench was empty. The playground was deserted. A forgotten soccer ball lay near the swings.

From this vantage point, you could clearly see the two circles Joey had made in the dirt about twenty or thirty feet apart from one another. Below each one, there were bunches of short lines. A faint wavy line scalloped around the edges of the playground. I could see two small triangles on the far side of the wavy circle. Other random lines curved below us. There definitely seemed to be a pattern to what Joey had drawn. . . .

And then the picture suddenly became clear.

"Oh!" Veena and I gasped, seeing it at the exact same time.

The face of a Marshallville Tiger was staring up at us.

JOEYBYRD

Joey had worked on the design in his head all week. It was the biggest tracing he'd done yet. When drawing a giant tiger face (or anything else), the order of the lines was the most important part. One line had to lead to the next.

You couldn't walk all the way from the ears to the mouth, for instance, unless you wanted to waste a lot of time and make a lot of extra footprints that went nowhere and meant nothing.

Joey didn't like wasting time or footprints.

Inside his head, he'd given a number to each part of the tiger. The wavy fur around the outside of the tiger's face was number 1. The triangle ears were numbers 2 and 3. A stripe below them was 4. And so on.

On Friday, all he had to do was keep track of the time and follow the order of the numbers in his head—kind of like the paint-by-numbers horse he got from his grandparents one Christmas. Only he wasn't making a horse. Or using paint.

Number 21 was his last number.

It was the nose.

When he got to that part, he had only three minutes left. Trying to be as fast as he could, Joey zipped up his red coat and lay down in the middle of his tracing. He ignored the blazing sun on his face and all the scratchy bits of bark digging into his back.

Angling his arms like the sides of a triangle, he let out a deep sighing breath. A sensation like floating or soaring flowed through him. This was his favorite part: The moment when the wind and the sky wrapped around him. The moment when he felt like he could fly.

In his mind, he could see everything below him—the huge tiger's face with its rippling orange-and-black fur, its glowing eyes, its fierce mouth, and its warm red nose.

It was so perfect, so real—if he listened closely, he could almost hear the tiger roar.

April: One Question Leads to Another

Veena and I shook our heads at the sight.

"Wow. I just can't believe that," I said.

Smiling softly, Mr. Ulysses took his foot off the ledge and turned to squint at me. "So what do you think about our friend Joey now?"

"I don't know," I had to admit.

Part of me felt kind of stunned. How had Joey been able to create something this large, this perfect—something he couldn't even *see*—using only his feet? And while wearing Crocs, for goodness' sake?

The other part of me was mad.

I wanted to drag every person who had ever called Joey a traitor or a moron—or anything else—up to the roof to see the fantastic tiger he'd done for our Spirit Day. Maybe they'd think twice before mocking kids like him again. Maybe they'd learn not to jump to conclusions about people. Maybe a few kids would actually (gasp!) be interested in being friends with him now—since he'd proven he was a loyal Tigers fan. Not that it should matter. . . .

Mr. Ulysses chuckled. "Sometimes one question leads to another, doesn't it?"

"How did he do it?" asked Veena, studying the design intently.

Mr. Ulysses shrugged. "Beats the heck out of me. That's the million-dollar question, isn't it? I watched him make it, and I still have no idea how he managed it."

It occurred to me that maybe we weren't the only people the janitor had allowed on the roof. "Has Joey ever been up here?" I asked.

Mr. Ulysses shook his head. "Nope. But I wondered the same thing when I first saw what he was doing. I thought to myself—was it possible the little kid was sneaking up here somehow and mapping all this out? But I keep the boiler room locked when I'm not there, and I'm the only one who's got the keys." He pulled a very official-looking ring of keys out of his pocket and jangled them. "Here they are. Haven't left my sight in years."

Around us, the roof shimmered with questions and heat. I could feel a slow trickle of moisture running down the middle of my back. Although there was a slight breeze, the black-tar roof was getting hotter by the minute. A shine of sweat glistened on Veena's forehead.

I definitely wanted to stay longer, but I didn't want to look like a pool of sweat when I got back to class. Plus, I was concerned about how much class time we were missing.

Mr. Ulysses seemed to read my mind. "Well, I think we'd better wrap up today's field trip and get you both back to class, right?"

"Yes." Veena nodded. I could tell she was getting as anxious as me.

I have to admit that it was pretty fun to descend from the roof into the boiler room. I felt like a star in an action thriller as we climbed through the trapdoor opening, one by one. Skipping the last two rungs of the ladder, I jumped to the concrete floor and landed (sort of) gracefully on my feet.

Tanner Torchman would have been impressed.

After Veena reached the bottom of the ladder, Mr. Ulysses followed more slowly. With a grunt, he yanked the trapdoor closed and made his way carefully down the rungs. When he got to the floor, he took a deep breath and wiped his arm across his red face. "Whew, it was pretty warm up there today"—and then he smacked his forehead. "Doggone it. I knew there was something I forgot to do while we were up there."

"What?" I asked.

"I wanted to get a better picture of the tiger for my collection."

I looked at Mr. Ulysses incredulously. "You have pictures?"

Mr. Ulysses grinned. "Of course."

April: Polaroids

Turns out Mr. Ulysses had an entire *drawerful* of Joey's work.

He pulled open the center drawer of his old wooden desk, and it was stuffed with dozens of square cards made of white plastic.

"Are those photographs?" Veena asked, leaning closer.

"Yep." Mr. Ulysses nodded. "They're Polaroids. The pictures print right out of the camera. A couple of years ago, I got one of those old cameras from a teacher who was retiring. Ron Blanchard. Good guy. They don't make teachers like that anymore." He nodded toward an odd-looking object sitting on a shelf near his desk, as if it was Mr. Blanchard himself. "That's the one that belonged to him."

It looked more like a toy than a real camera. I made a mental note to research more about Polaroids when I had the chance.

"It's practically an antique, but it works great. See for yourself." Mr. Ulysses reached into his desk and pulled out a handful of the white cards. He handed one to Veena and one to me. Although it felt like plastic, I was surprised to see that mine actually had a color picture on it. A very blurry image of Joey's tiger.

"See, that's the one I wanted to retake." Mr. Ulysses pointed at mine. "My hand moved."

He tapped the photo in Veena's hands, which showed a big spiral around the 2003 Tree. "Now that one is a lot more common. Today was the first time I've ever seen him make a tiger, but he does a lot of circles and spirals like the ones you're holding. Not sure why."

"It reminds me of some of our art in India," Veena commented, holding the photo closer to study it.

Mr. Ulysses shuffled through more photos in his hands. "Actually, I've got a ton of Joey's spiral photos. Big ones. Small ones. In fact, I think a couple of these might have been from last spring by the look of the tree."

I glanced up in surprise. "Joey was doing them last spring?"

Mr. Ulysses nodded.

"Has he been making designs longer than that?" Veena asked.

Mr. Ulysses shook his head. "Don't think so. He moved here at the start of third grade, I believe." He squinted upward. "His family came from Illinois or Indiana, I think."

He continued. "In fact, I only noticed what he was doing because I was up on the roof one afternoon, fixing a problem with the roof drain over the art room. He'd made a giant face that day. Frowning." Mr. Ulysses chuckled. "When I first saw it, I thought my eyes were playing tricks, let me tell you. Looking down and seeing the playground frowning at me—that definitely got my attention."

Veena spoke up. "Did you ask him about it?"

"Yep." The janitor nodded. "But I didn't get very far. When I asked him if he was unhappy about something, he got this scared look and took off. After that, he avoided me like the plague. I didn't bother him again, but that's when I started taking pictures of whatever he drew. I thought somebody ought to be saving it." He paused. "I know I probably should have shown the pictures to Mr. Mac or one of his teachers, but I guess I kept hoping that maybe they'd notice things on their own."

He passed another Polaroid snapshot to us. The lines on the playground resembled an unraveling ball of yarn.

"See, sometimes he does a bunch of scrambled lines and I can't figure out what the heck he's making. Maybe he just wanders around like that when he can't think of anything to do," the janitor said.

"But here are some of my all-time favorites." He handed us three more photos. One had a splotch of dried mustard on it, as if Mr. Ulysses had kept it on his desk at some point. It showed a person's face looking up from the playground. The person appeared to be bald with a round, yelling mouth that filled half of his face.

I squinted more closely at it. "Is that supposed to be Mr. Dunner?"

Mr. Ulysses coughed and seemed to hide a grin. "Don't know. Maybe."

The gym teacher was well known for yelling. He liked to announce on a daily basis: "I HAVE THE LOUDEST VOICE IN THIS SCHOOL. DON'T MAKE ME USE IT." He was my least favorite teacher at Marshallville. To be fair, a gym teacher would never be my favorite teacher, no matter what—but still, Mr. Dunner yelled *a lot*.

From the photo, it was pretty obvious that Joey felt the same way I did about the guy.

Another picture showed what appeared to be waves covering the playground.

"Waves?" Veena asked, holding the picture closer.

"Yep, I think so. Not sure why he did them that day." Mr. Ulysses handed us another photo. "But can you guess this one?"

It looked like a wagon wheel with small circles inside it. Veena and I both tried turning the photo upside down and then right side up to figure it out. "Okay, we give up," I said finally. "What is it?"

The janitor laughed. "Ha. That one's tricky. It took me a while too. He made it this past Wednesday. Pizza day." He pointed to the dots on the wagon wheel. "Pepperoni."

Pizza Day. *The day Joey had jumped around like an obsessed rabbit and spun in circles.*

Wow.

Veena and I burst out laughing at the same time.

"That is so . . ." I searched my mind for a word that fit. The only thing I could think of was "amazing"—which is such an overused word that it doesn't work to describe things that actually *are* amazing—but it was the best one I could come up with.

"Amazing," I said.

As I studied the photos in my hands, I felt a shiver of excitement. I loved discovering things. And it felt as if we'd just made a rare discovery in the old boiler room of Marshallville Elementary: a previously unknown species of student, a mysterious fourth-grade artist, a creative genius. . . .

"Why hasn't anyone else figured out what he's doing?" I wondered out loud.

Every recess, there were at least a hundred kids on the playground. Plus Mrs. Zeff. Sometimes a teacher came outside too. Joey had been doing his tracings since last year, according to Mr. Ulysses. Why hadn't anyone noticed what he was doing? When the drawings were *right there in front of them*? It seemed impossible.

"I wondered the same thing," Mr. Ulysses agreed.

"It's so obvious once you see it."

"Yes." The janitor nodded. "It is."

And then he added after a thoughtful pause, "However, I came to the conclusion a long time ago that people often see only what they expect to see. If they don't expect much, they don't see much."

Was he talking about himself? I wondered. About being a janitor?

"Or they see all the things they don't like," Veena added. "And then they ignore everything else."

"Exactly." Mr. Ulysses nodded.

He sat down in his sagging office chair again. "So you two are much smarter people than me. What do you think we should do with what we know? Should we share it? Or stay quiet and keep it to ourselves? That's the dilemma."

To speak or not to speak went through my mind.

"I think people *must* find out about him," Veena replied with absolute conviction. "He is an extremely gifted person. Everyone must see his gifts. I think he will be quite famous."

The janitor's gaze shifted to me. "April . . . your thoughts?"

I wasn't so sure.

Normally, I was the kind of person who would jump into things, especially if I thought there was a way I could help out or make something better.

Yes, I wanted Joey Byrd to get the respect he deserved.

And okay, maybe a small part of me wanted outcasts *in general* to get the respect they deserved—and maybe that included me.

But could the idea backfire somehow? Did Joey really want everyone to know about his playground art? And what would happen when they did?

"I don't know," I said after a long hesitation. "I see what Veena is saying, but I think we need to know a little more first. Like what Joey wants. And what his drawings actually mean." I handed the photos back to Mr. Ulysses.

Veena seemed to agree.

"Good. Then it's settled." Mr. Ulysses nodded. "For now, we say nothing. I'll write you some hall passes to get back to class." He pushed the handful of Polaroid photos into his desk and closed the squeaky drawer. "Our lips are sealed."

JOEYBYRD

A lot of things looked much better from above. Joey kept
a list of them in his head:
   Large tiger faces
   Pretzels
   Keyboards
   Circus tents
   Open umbrellas
   Winding rivers
   And the colorful bowls of Kellogg's Froot Loops cereal
that Joey ate for breakfast every morning.

April: More Clues

We knew about Joey's secret gift, and at the same time we had to pretend we didn't know about it. It was a tough spot to be in.

I could tell Veena desperately wanted to talk to Joey at recess. And I wanted to ask him a whole list of questions that I'd been jotting down in my notebook. Such as: How did he map out the giant drawings? Why did he make them? Where did he get his ideas from? Why did he keep his tracings a secret?

But I felt like we had to wait for the right moment. We couldn't act too curious—or he'd start to avoid us. We couldn't draw too much attention to him—or other people would start to notice.

Just by coincidence, I happened to meet Joey's parents at Open House a couple of days after we saw the tiger. Every year, Marshallville Elementary held an Open House in the middle of September for parents to meet their kids' teachers. They always asked sixth graders to volunteer to help—to be *ambassadors* for the school—so I had signed up.

Anyway, I was working at the Open House registration

table when Joey's parents came over to get their name tags and classroom assignments. I don't know what I expected them to look like, but they had zero resemblance to Joey. Like, if you were playing a matching game with parents and kids, you would never put them together at first.

Joey's mom was a large-sized woman with long hair pulled back in a braid. Although her face didn't look that old, her hair was almost entirely gray. She wasn't dressed up like some of the other moms were for Open House. She was wearing a hospital scrubs–type top with bears on it and pink pants and white sneakers. Maybe she was a nurse.

Joey's dad was tall and thin with thick-lens glasses. He had dark hair that kept falling across his forehead, and he kept nervously pushing it away every few seconds. That was the only detail that reminded me slightly of Joey and some of his habits.

Joey's mom did all the talking. "Hello. We're the parents of Joey Byrd. He's in the fourth grade," she said in a rehearsed kind of way. His dad nodded.

Searching the table for their name tags, I spotted the one for Joey's mom first. She was called Denise. An ordinary name, right?

But his dad was called Nibor—a name I'd never heard before.

"That's an interesting name. Like 'neighbor,'" I commented, just to be friendly.

"Yes," Joey's dad replied without smiling. He didn't

share any more details about it, and I felt kind of embarrassed for saying something.

The other unusual thing I noticed about Joey's parents was the fact that they didn't put on their name tags right away, like most parents do. Joey's dad carefully folded his tag in half, creasing it with a fingernail. Then he shoved it into his shirt pocket. Joey's mom tucked hers into the front of her purse.

Why did they hide them? I wondered. Were they ashamed of Joey—or of being his parents? Or were they like Joey—did they prefer being unknown and invisible too?

I couldn't imagine my parents acting the same way. Not in a million years. My parents had the opposite problem—they were always saying too much about me in public. My dad would tell perfect strangers how I was a straight-A student, or how I'd been in the newspaper for something. My mom had a button with my picture and the words "Marshallville Honor Student" emblazoned across it. It was pretty embarrassing. She wore it everywhere.

"Is there a schedule for tonight?" Joey's mom asked, glancing uncertainly at all the stacks of paperwork on the table.

"Sure." As I handed her one of the printed schedules and pointed out the parts that related to the fourth grade, Joey's dad kind of wandered off by himself. I couldn't really tell what he was doing, but I could see him standing at the end of the registration table.

Once I finished explaining the schedule, Joey's mom

motioned impatiently at him. "Come on, Nibor. We've got to get going before all the seats are taken."

After they left, I noticed that Joey's dad had arranged most of the pens on the registration table into five letters. They spelled out the word "ROBIN."

It took me a minute to get it. Then, I cracked up. *Nibor (Robin) Byrd.* It was pretty clever actually. Was it his dad's real name? Who knows . . . but I was definitely starting to see where Joey got his creativity from.

When I shared the story with Veena the next day, both of us laughed about it.

That same week, she managed to get a better glimpse of the gold disk that Joey wore around his neck all the time. "I just happened to be standing next to him in the office yesterday, so I got a really good look at it. I'm pretty sure it's a compass, not a watch," she said. "It had arrows and letters on it."

We decided maybe Joey used it for mapping his designs.

For most of the week we did okay at keeping quiet about Joey. However, Mr. Mac nearly gave us a heart attack when he asked about him in front of the whole group on Friday.

We were having our usual Buddy Bench meeting. A bag of Oreos was slowly making its way around the table when he suddenly turned to me. "So what's up with our fourth-grade daydreamer these days, April? Any new revelations about Joey Byrd?"

Veena gave an audible gasp, and her hand froze inside

the Oreo bag. The two Rs looked at her oddly. Somehow I managed to answer, "No, everything's fine. He seems okay." Then I shoved an Oreo into my mouth to keep from having to reveal anything else.

"We spend a lot of time making friendship bracelets with the girls," Veena added quickly.

"Gosh, we hate those stupid things," Rochelle said, snorting. "The third graders are making them too. It drives us crazy. 'Tie this for me.' 'Thread this for me,'" she mimicked.

Veena had a couple of the colorful bracelets on her wrist. She quietly slid her hand off the table and into her lap. Mr. Mac, as usual, didn't catch on. He started describing all the fads he'd seen in school over the years—slime, fidget spinners, wheelie shoes—and the topic of Joey was (thankfully) forgotten.

Fortunately, Joey seemed oblivious to us.

He'd made his usual spirals and circles and wandering squiggles that week, except for one recess when he drew what we thought was an owl—although we weren't sure why.

Mr. Ulysses took a picture of it from the rooftop.

JOEYBYRD

It is almost impossible to surprise an owl. It can turn its head 270 degrees in either direction—even though it prefers not to. It has three eyelids. One is see-through.

Joey didn't need to turn his head 270 degrees, or look through his eyelids, to know he was being watched by the sixth-grade girl with the notebook and the new girl from another country. Everywhere he went, he could feel their prickling gaze on his back.

Joey made the owl for two reasons. First, to show the girls that he was watching them. Second, to show the girls that they couldn't surprise him.

But then—surprisingly—they did.

April: The Circle Makers

"There are other people like him!"

Although it was a Monday—a day she didn't work—Veena showed up at the Buddy Bench at the start of recess.

I turned toward her, only half hearing what she said at first. I had the hood of my coat pulled up because it was windy and absolutely freezing outside. "Why the heck are you out here?" I asked, looking at Veena like she was nuts. "You aren't even supposed to be working today."

The fifth grader was wearing a thin grape-colored hoodie and striped leggings. The wind whipped her dark hair around. Sitting down next to me, she bounced her striped knees up and down to keep warm.

"I know, but I had to show you what I found this weekend!" Her voice stayed on warp speed. Pulling a phone out of her pocket, she flicked through it.

"Look!" Trembling from the cold or excitement (or both), she held the screen toward me.

I leaned closer. "What am I looking at?"

"The field," she replied impatiently.

On the screen, there was a picture of a green field. I held the phone closer. The photo rotated and shifted. I turned the phone to get the image back.

Finally I saw what Veena was talking about: a precise, perfect spiral in the middle of a field of green stalks.

"Wow. That's really cool," I said. "It's a corn maze just like Joey's designs."

"No." Veena shook her head emphatically. "It's not a maze. They are called 'crop circles.' It is a type of secret artwork. And not every design is a circle. I found a lot more examples."

She swiped through more pictures showing me outlines of giant white horses, elaborate labyrinths, intricate stars, bizarre geometric patterns, interlocking ring designs—and *lots* of spirals and circles. Some were in fields. Others were carved into hillsides. A few had been made on wide, sandy beaches.

I was pretty amazed. "How did you find all these pictures?"

Veena smiled. "Last night I was thinking about Joey's spirals and wondering if there were other people around the world who make big designs too. So, just for fun, I searched 'giant circle makers' on my phone, since that is what Joey does a lot of the time. And all of these photos came up." Veena's voice rose excitedly. "I couldn't believe it."

I tried not to look impressed, but I have to admit that I was. (And okay—I was also kind of jealous that she had thought of this idea before I did.)

"Crop circle designs are quite mysterious—that's what I learned," she continued. "According to what I read, they usually appear in the middle of the night. Often no one knows how they were made. Or who made them. Or why they appear in certain places and not others. Like in England near Stonehenge—they are seen quite often there."

"Stonehenge and Michigan?" I joked.

Without stopping for a breath, Veena kept chattering. "And the crops in the fields are always carefully flattened, not cut—so it isn't possible that a machine is making them. Some scientists think it might be a magnetic vortex, like a tornado, that creates some of them because people often experience a dizzy or tingling feeling near the designs."

Squinting skeptically, I held up the horse picture on Veena's phone again. "A magnetic vortex made this horse?"

"Maybe not." Veena smiled and shrugged. "Other people believe the designs are made by secret societies of artists called circle makers who pass down their skills and tools from generation to generation. But no one really knows for sure. It's a mystery." Her eyes shifted toward Joey.

At that moment, he was weaving slowly around the swing sets. Although the temperature was in the thirties, his coat was unzipped and he wasn't wearing any socks. I could see about two inches of his bone-white ankles sticking out below his pant legs.

"Do you think he might want to see my pictures too?" Veena asked. "Or maybe he knows about the circle makers already?"

"I guess we could try." I rubbed my cold nose, still feeling slightly envious of her discovery.

Getting up, we walked across the arctic tundra of the

playground. You could tell that Joey sensed our approach. His footsteps sped up. He turned in the opposite direction and veered toward the jungle gym to avoid us.

"You try talking to him first," Veena whispered.

"Hey, Joey," I called out when we got close enough.

The boy's eyes glanced suspiciously over his shoulder at us. I stepped over one of his lines, not wanting to mess up anything.

"Hey, we wanted to show you some cool pictures Veena found on her phone. They reminded us of the tracings you make sometimes. Do you want to see them?"

Joey's brown eyes stared at my face for a second or two, and I had the distinct feeling that he was trying to decide if he could trust what I was saying.

"Okay," he said suddenly, and the air around us exhaled.

Scuffing toward us, he held out his hand. "Let me see them."

"Here, I can show the pictures to you," Veena tried to insist. I could tell she was nervous about handing over her phone. It looked pretty new.

"Just give it to me," Joey said impatiently, still reaching.

Although Joey's hands weren't super clean, Veena finally gave up arguing. She handed over her nice phone. I think both of us held our breaths—not sure what would happen next—as Joey took it.

It felt like a long couple of minutes as Joey stared silently at the screen, but I'm sure it was only a few seconds. Once he realized what was on it, I swear you could literally see his eyes widen with amazement.

Without asking Veena for permission, he began swiping through more of the pictures she'd found, holding the phone just inches from his eyes. He almost seemed to be memorizing each picture. You could see a whole panorama of emotions—wonder, curiosity, surprise, fascination—flickering across his face.

Veena and I stayed quiet, stamping our feet up and down to keep warm, until Joey finally looked up again.

"Where are these?" were the first words he said to us.

"You mean where can you see them?" Veena asked.

Joey nodded.

"Well, I think a lot of them are in places like England, not here," she stammered. "But I believe they have been found in many other countries too."

"I definitely want to go to England then," Joey replied in a distant voice, as if he was already heading across the Atlantic in his mind.

"Actually, I don't think you can see them there right now," I attempted to explain. "A lot of them were created in fields, you know, so they aren't really permanent. They're like your tracings. They weren't made to last a long time. That's why people took pictures of them."

"It doesn't matter. I'm going to see them," Joey stubbornly insisted, setting his mouth in a firm line. "I want to meet other people who make spirals of sadness too."

"Spirals of sadness?" Veena and I repeated together, our voices tripping over one another.

Joey flicked through the pictures and held up the spiral in the green field. "This."

"Why do you call them spirals of sadness?" Veena's eyes darted nervously toward me. I could tell she was thinking the same thing I was: Were we asking him too many questions? Could we keep him talking to us?

Joey gave an audible sigh, as if we were as dumb as rocks.

"Because"—he started to walk in a tight coil, dragging his left sneaker through the dirt—"you think of something sad and you start walking. Then you think of more sad things and you walk. And you just keep walking and thinking of sad things." He kept walking, making a larger spiral in front of us. "Until the sad things finally go away."

A thick lump rose in my throat.

I didn't dare look over at Veena, because I knew she was probably feeling the exact same way. It was impossible not to remember all the spirals Mr. Ulysses had in his desk drawer. *I've got a ton of his spiral photos,* the janitor had told us. Then there were the ones Joey had put in my Advice Box the year before. Plus the spiral he'd left this year— the one I'd thought was an exploding solar system.

In other words, most of Joey's art was sadness. Which was really sad to think about.

"I'm not lying. It works." Joey glared at the two of us, as if he thought we were mocking him somehow.

"No. We believe you," I finally managed to say. "But we seriously had no idea what your spirals meant. If we had known how you were feeling and how upset you were, we would have tried to do something to help you out."

Next to me, Veena nodded.

Joey crossed his arms as if he was about to have a complete meltdown. A glaze of tears shone in his eyes. "I'm not lying. It works," he repeated, looking more frustrated with us. Clearly, we weren't getting through to him.

"Honestly, we believe you," I repeated. "That's what I'm trying to tell you."

"Then you try it." Joey ducked his head down and continued his spiral walk. "You try it and see."

JOEYBYRD

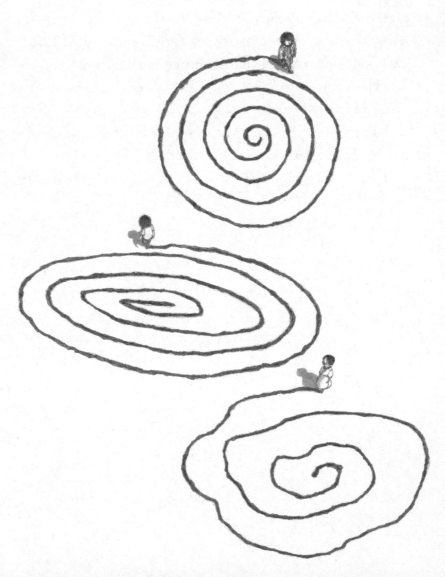

April: Walking in Circles

It is not easy to walk in a perfect spiral while thinking about sad things. It may sound simple, but it isn't.

First off, I couldn't stop worrying about the sixth graders in the cafeteria. Were they watching me walk in circles and laughing hysterically? Second, I couldn't seem to coordinate my eyes and my feet to make evenly spaced lines in the dirt. The more I walked, the more my spiral looked like a deformed egg.

Out of the corner of my eye, I checked how Veena was doing.

She was about ten feet away from me, scuffing her left shoe through the wood chips. Her flimsy ballet flat barely left a mark, but she stubbornly kept going. Since her face was concealed by her purple hoodie, I couldn't see her expression. Was she thinking about her old life in India? I wondered. Was she lonely here? Did she feel like a stranger in Marshallville? In America? Had she wanted to come here?

Although I often imagined how great it would be to move somewhere else and be someone totally different, was that true? Would I want to be like Veena and leave everything behind?

To be honest, I started running out of sad things to think about in my own life after about five minutes.

Once I'd gotten past losing Julie as a friend . . . and not having made another friend yet . . . and always feeling like an outsider in sixth grade . . . and my brother being in his own world and ignoring me these days . . . and our older cat, Patches, having to be put to sleep last year, which was *terrible* . . . I couldn't come up with much else. . . .

So I started thinking about bigger problems from the outside world, like war, terrorism, violence, school shootings, global warming, animals going extinct, earthquakes, hurricanes, floods—and it became pretty clear that the outside world has a *lot* more sadness than my own life. Which kind of puts things in perspective, you know?

Weirdly, the longer I walked, the calmer I felt. And colder.

Calmer, but colder.

Once I decided my lopsided spiral was finished, I told Joey how his idea really seemed to work. "I liked it a lot," I said. "Would you mind if I wrote about it in my advice column someday? I think it could help other kids."

He replied with a vague shrug. "I guess. But your spiral is crooked," he added, pointing at mine. "And nobody can see yours," he said to Veena.

Hers resembled the faint imprint of a fossil shell.

"At least it's better than mine," I joked, and Veena smiled.

Truthfully, our spirals didn't really matter. What was

more important was the fact that Joey Byrd was finally opening up and talking to us.

Talking.

Of course, the recess bell rang before we could ask him any more questions. Without another word, Joey took off for the back doors of the school, leaving us standing next to our spirals of sadness.

My nose was running from the cold. Veena's teeth were chattering. Still, it felt like we'd taken a major step forward. We'd started to figure out more about Joey Byrd.

Unfortunately, just as I'd feared—other people had noticed us (and Joey) too.

April: Inevitable

On Wednesday, a small bunch of the bracelet-making girls strolled toward us. Recess had been indoors on Tuesday because of rain, so this was our first day outside since making the spirals with Joey. The weather was still cold and damp. Just by the expressions on the girls' faces, I could tell something was up.

"Watch out. Here comes some big drama," I whispered to Veena, who was so bundled up against the cold, I don't think she heard a word.

"What?" she said, pushing down the hood of her coat.

I waved my hand. "Never mind."

The tall girl at the front of the group spoke up first. Her name was Alanna, but I called her the Bossy One in my head. Despite her pushy personality, all the fourth-grade girls seemed to look up to her. I don't know if it was because she wore designer clothes and stylish Ugg boots, but she had more friendship bracelets than anyone.

"So we have a question for you, Veena," she started out saying in this singsong voice.

The other girls glanced at each other and giggled.

"Yes?" Veena answered patiently. She was always way more patient with the fourth graders than I was.

"Well, we don't want to be rude, but . . ." There was an extra-dramatic pause. "We want to know . . . is Joey Byrd your *boyfriend* now?" The whole group dissolved into uproarious laughter.

What? Veena looked shocked by the question. I was kind of shocked too. Where was this idea coming from? We stared blankly at one another for a second or so.

Finally, Veena answered slowly, "No. Why do you say that?"

"Well"—Alanna tilted her head coyly—"first we noticed you spent most of recess on Monday talking to Joey. When we asked him about it later on, he said he liked you a lot. I mean, like, *a lot*. He said he thought you were *very beautiful*." More uproarious laughter. "So we thought you had to be boyfriend and girlfriend."

I could feel my irritation rising fast.

If they had picked on Joey, or teased him in *any* way, I swear I would go straight to Ms. Getzhammer. I gave the Bossy One a withering glare. "Actually, *both of us* talked to him on Monday. That's what we do for the Buddy Bench. We talk to fourth graders and help out when you guys need it. That's our job. And I'm warning all of you"—I pointed at the group—"you better leave Joey alone and stop bothering him about stupid stuff like boyfriends and girlfriends. Got it?"

Mouths open, the girls gawked at me, as if I'd come across as kind of harsh.

Then Veena made the problem *much* worse.

"Yes," she added in this innocent voice. "Most people

don't know this about Joey, but he is quite talented at art. In other parts of the world, people who make designs like him are called circle makers."

What? My head snapped toward Veena.

"What?" the girls replied, looking confused.

Alanna pushed back her fur-lined hood and squinted in Joey's direction. He was standing by himself near the swing sets. "Circles? What do you mean?" she said. "I don't see any circles on the playground."

Without pausing, Veena reached into her coat pocket for her phone. "Here—I will you show you some pictures to explain," she replied.

Oh my gosh. What was she doing?

I literally couldn't get a single syllable out of my mouth before Veena had started passing around her phone showing off the same photos from Monday. I wasn't sure if she was doing this to distract everyone from the boyfriend-girlfriend conversation . . . or if she was trying to impress the girls . . . or if she honestly didn't realize the disaster she was causing.

Of course, the girls oohed and aahed over the designs. They flipped back and forth through the pictures as they handed the phone around. "Wow, that is so cool," they said. "That one is my favorite. I love the horse. How did an artist do that?"

At some point, while all of this was happening, I think Veena must have realized that she had made a huge mistake. (Or maybe she caught the look of complete shock on my face.)

She tried to make up a flimsy excuse.

"Okay, I need to put my phone away now—thank you," she said, reaching desperately for it. "I don't want to run down the battery. Could you pass it back to me, please?"

"So I don't get it," Alanna said as the phone made its way back around the circle. "Joey didn't really make any of those designs you showed us, did he?"

Glancing at me, Veena now looked absolutely terrified.

Instead of answering, she just shook her head and tucked her chin inside her zipped-up coat. Her dark hair fell over her glasses, completely hiding her eyes behind a curtain of hair.

That left me to answer the question.

Alanna turned her pointed gaze toward me. "So did he make them or not?"

There was literally no way out. The Bossy One would get an answer, one way or another.

"No, he didn't make the ones in the photos," I replied carefully. "He usually does—well, uh, he does his own designs."

Alanna looked unconvinced. "Where?"

"Sometimes here on the playground," I admitted reluctantly. "Or other places," I added, although I had no idea if that was true.

Alanna gazed across the playground, surveying everything skeptically. The other girls followed her lead. "I don't see him making anything," she said.

Joey was wandering near the jungle gym now, aimlessly scuffing at the dirt.

"Well, actually, nobody can see what he's making unless you are really high up." I gestured vaguely toward the slate-gray sky. "And he doesn't make a drawing every day. So you'll just have to wait until he makes one again—and who knows when that will happen?" I shrugged.

If I thought my vague and evasive answer would satisfy the girls and convince them to give up on Joey—it didn't. Before recess ended, the rumors about Joey and his playground art were already spreading like wildfire.

April: The Cat Is out of the Bag

After recess I knew I had to track down Mr. Ulysses to tell him the whole story. We had promised to keep Joey's art a secret—and we hadn't.

Surprisingly, he wasn't as worried as I thought he'd be.

I found him in the cafeteria sweeping up after lunch. Big mounds of lunch garbage were scattered everywhere. I didn't want to interrupt his work, so I tried to talk quickly.

I told Mr. Ulysses how Joey's secret had come out accidentally—putting most of the blame on the bracelet girls rather than Veena. I knew she already felt guilty enough—she'd run inside the school without saying a word after the conversation with the girls had ended.

"Hmmm." The janitor gazed up at the ceiling after I finished. "So it seems that the cat is out of the bag now, isn't it?"

I winced. "I guess."

"No way of putting a cat back in, right?"

"I guess not."

"Then it seems that all we can do is wait and see what happens next." Mr. Ulysses pushed a loose candy wrapper into a nearby pile with his foot. He smiled. "Who knows? It could turn out to be a good thing after all."

His optimism surprised me. "How?"

Mr. Ulysses shrugged. "You can never tell where a simple line may lead. The greatest things have often come from the simplest lines."

I squinted at him. "What do you mean?"

"Well." He glanced upward. "Take something like poetry. That's all made up of lines. Or think about art. Or the maps of epic journeys. Or strands of DNA. Or the span of human history. You name it"—Mr. Ulysses waved one hand in the air—"all of them started with a single line."

I'll admit I'd never thought of this really interesting idea before.

Like I said, sometimes Mr. Ulysses notices things that absolutely nobody else does. It is another one of the qualities I like best about him.

Pushing his broom toward one of the garbage piles again, the janitor winked at me. "Don't panic. I think everything will turn out fine for Joey."

"Okay," I replied, not entirely convinced it would.

But all the way back to class I kept thinking about what Mr. Ulysses had said: *You can never tell where a simple line may lead.* . . .

And I hoped he was right.

JOEYBYRD

The next day, Joey could tell that something had definitely changed at recess. And not in a good way. He did the only thing he could think of to protect himself.

He lay down flat on the playground and closed his eyes.

April: Surrounded

Revealing Joey's secret to the bracelet girls definitely didn't lead to something positive at first, despite what Mr. Ulysses had predicted. Even before I reached the playground on Thursday, I heard the commotion. Two fourth-grade girls passed me in the hallway.

One said to the other: "I told you it was a lie."

The other replied, "Yeah, I knew that story about him was fake."

The first girl shook her head. "What a dork."

My stomach gave a sickening lurch. I knew they were talking about Joey.

I'd planned to get outside early. I had a feeling some of the bracelet girls might pick on Joey, or bug him about drawing something, and I'd already decided to keep an eye on him for the entire recess to make sure they left him alone.

But we had a substitute for language arts, and he'd kept us for an extra few minutes past the lunch bell. By the time I pushed open the glass doors to the playground and charged outside, it was already too late.

I saw it all in one sweeping glance: Joey lying on the

ground with his eyes closed. Mrs. Zeff and another teacher shooing a big group away from him. "Stop bothering Joey or we'll give all of you a detention," they were shouting. "Go somewhere else and play. You're wasting your own recess time." As the kids took off toward the sports fields, I could see some phones reluctantly disappearing into coat pockets. Usually the fourth graders didn't have phones or bring them outside for recess, so I knew they'd done it to capture whatever Joey was doing.

I felt horrible. Literally, I felt sick to my stomach seeing Joey on the ground and all the kids running away like a pack of wolves. Although I had no idea how to fix the mess, I forced myself to walk over to where Joey was lying. The least I could do was to apologize.

"Hey, Joey."

Even though the ground was cold and damp, I sat cross-legged on the ground right next to him. "It's April— I'm the one who made the spirals with you on Monday," I added, because Joey's eyes were still closed. They weren't clenched shut, just peacefully closed—the kind of creepy dead look he often liked to do.

"Are you okay?" I asked.

Joey's head nodded almost imperceptibly.

"Do you want me to help you get up?"

His head shook back and forth emphatically. NO.

"Is it okay if I sit here and talk to you for a couple of minutes?"

No answer.

By now Mrs. Zeff had moved to another part of the playground. Except for a few stragglers, most of the fourth graders were playing on the sports fields. Nobody else was around. I zipped up my jacket because it felt like it could pour at any minute. Angry clouds scudded across the sky. I took a deep breath and let it out slowly.

Confession wasn't getting any easier.

"Okay," I said finally. "I know you are probably confused about what happened today and how everybody knew about your tracings." I swallowed hard. "I have to be honest that I think it was my fault and Veena's fault. Some of the fourth-grade girls asked about your tracings yesterday, and we made a big mistake and told them more than we should have."

Joey didn't open his eyes or give any sign that he was listening.

I sighed loudly. "I know it was a really, really stupid thing for us to do. I'm mad at myself because I know you trusted us, and we should have just shut up. And I'm really sorry if all the kids swarmed around you today and made you scared—or if they were mean to you. We had no idea it would get out of hand like this."

I paused because my voice was starting to wobble. "After recess is over, I promise I'll talk to Mr. Mac or Ms. Getzhammer, and I swear I'll make sure it doesn't happen again."

Joey's eyelids fluttered a little, but he didn't answer.

"Do you accept my apology?" I had to ask.

His chin bobbed up and down slightly.

"Do you want me to leave you alone?"

This time his lips moved. One word came out: "Yes."

I swallowed again, feeling *even worse*, if that was possible.

"Okay. I'll go ahead and stop bothering you. But I just want to apologize again for what happened. Veena and I think you are a really cool person who does amazing drawings—or tracings, as you call them. You're like . . ." I searched my mind for the right words. "A star to us."

No reaction. Joey's eyes stayed closed.

Sighing loudly, I stood up and brushed the dirt off the back of my jeans. Shoving my hands deep into my coat pockets, I started walking toward the far end of the playground. I just wanted to be alone for a while.

Once I reached the edge of the playground area, I stood there for fifteen minutes probably, arms crossed, staring at nothing and being mad.

I was sick of Pokémon and plastic friendship bracelets and Buddy Benches and recess—and just all the stupid stuff in elementary school.

I wanted to be somewhere else. And older.

It took me a while to calm down. When I finally did, I turned around again. Of course, nothing much had changed. Marshallville Elementary was still there. Recess was still going on. I was still a sixth grader.

But I was relieved to see Joey had gotten up. He seemed to be back to his usual routine. He was making something in the middle of the playground. As I watched him, he walked in a diagonal line toward the 2003 Tree.

Nobody seemed to be bothering him. One small group of boys watched him from near the jungle gym. Two girls stood on the swings to get a better view of what he doing. Joey didn't seem to notice them or care.

When he got close to the tree, he pivoted and walked in another diagonal line. Then he stopped and pivoted again, walking in a straight line that crossed over his first one.

The boys near the jungle gym began climbing the rusty rungs for a better view. As one boy reached the peak, I heard him shout to the others that it looked like Joey was making an arrow. The words drifted toward me on the wind. "I'm pretty sure it's an arrow. That's what I definitely think it is."

Joey kept walking and pivoting, walking and pivoting, until he returned to the spot where he'd started. The jungle gym group figured it out before I did—

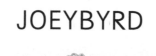

JOEYBYRD

April: Star Magic

"It's a star!" came the triumphant shout from the boys on the jungle gym.

I felt this warm glow of surprise. Had Joey made the star because of what I'd said to him—because I'd called him a star? Was it his way of making up to me and saying that everything was okay?

Unfortunately, I didn't get the chance to take a picture or get a better look at what Joey had drawn. Before I could walk over to see his tracing, the skies suddenly opened up and it began to pour. Heavy sheets of rain pummeled the playground. Yanking my coat over my head, I dashed toward the playground doors with everyone else.

Of course, all of us got totally soaked.

Once I got inside, I turned around to make sure Joey had come in—because you could never be sure what he would do. After I spotted his familiar jacket in the crowd, I headed back to my locker to dry off and hang up my things.

I'll be honest, I didn't really give the star a second thought. I had a quiz coming up in science, so I was kind of focused on that.

But then something unexpected happened.

Word of Joey's star started to spread after recess. A blurry photo of a large and impressive star began circulating through the school. On phones. On laptops. It was posted on our school district's Facebook page and Twitter feed sometime in the afternoon.

Oddly, the image in the photo seemed way more detailed than what Joey had been working on. When I first saw the photo, I wasn't convinced the star was the same one. How would Joey have had the time to make something so elaborate before the rain started?

I thought it was possible that Mr. Ulysses had posted the picture—and maybe he'd substituted a star that Joey had drawn on another day. Just to amaze people. That was only a guess, because I couldn't find the janitor to ask him.

All I can say for sure is that the rumors about Joey's star continued to grow as the afternoon went on. Opinions about it varied greatly, depending on who you talked to and what grade they were in.

Among the sixth graders, the star barely got noticed.

In the lower grades, it became a wondrous spectacle: *Someone had made the most beautiful star in the world on the school playground at recess!*

The real photo didn't really matter to the little kids. They had their own ideas of what the star had looked like: It had eight points, or twelve points, or—if you asked a kindergarten kid—"a hundred million points." It had rays like the sun. It had this bizarre—possibly magical—sparkle when it was finished. It was magical. Joey was magical. He had made the star with magic. Then he had made the rain to hide the magic. . . .

Okay, you can see how the story got a little out of control in the lower grades.

Regardless of the details, Joey's star took on a life of its own. By the time the buses arrived at the end of the day, the star had become a star.

Not surprisingly, my mom spotted it on Facebook.

When I got home from school, the first thing she said to me was: "Hey, I loved that picture the school district posted on its Facebook page today. The big star. What a creative idea to make giant pictures on the playground like that! I didn't know you could draw in wood chips. Did you get the chance to see it before the rain started?"

I had to stop myself from saying, "Yes, Mom, I've been trying to tell you about the kid who does them for, like, weeks now. And yes, as a matter of fact, I was there."

April: Captive Audience

On Friday, the hallways of Marshallville Elementary still buzzed with excitement about Joey.

On the way to my locker in the morning, I overheard a lot of speculation about what Joey would do next. Two little kids behind me decided it would *definitely* be something from *Star Wars*, although I thought it was pretty unlikely that Joey would re-create Darth Vader or the *Millennium Falcon* in wood chips.

As I passed the fourth-grade classrooms, I noticed that someone (probably Joey's teacher) had printed out the picture of his star. It was taped on the door of his classroom with the words: *Check out our amazing classroom star!* written above it.

I couldn't help smiling. Almost overnight, Joey had gone from an outcast in the hallway to a classroom star. Maybe there was some justice in the world after all.

Below the surface, I felt a little uneasy, though. I couldn't help worrying: What would Joey do on the playground today? What would the other kids do? Would Joey make another star? Or something else?

It was a Spirit Day, so I thought there was a small

possibility he might think of trying another tiger. Imagine how impressed everyone would be with that, right?

But I knew it was also possible he would do one of his spirals of sadness instead, and nobody would understand what it meant or how serious it was.

Right before the lunch periods started, the loudspeaker crackled. "Happy Spirit Day, Marshallville Elementary!" Ms. Getzhammer began. "With all the rain we've had, I've decided the sports fields are too wet for the teams to use, so everyone will be restricted to the playground area for today's recess," she said. "Behave appropriately."

A loud chorus of groans echoed through the school.

I wasn't sure whether to be relieved by the news or not. Ms. Getzhammer's decision meant Joey probably wouldn't have enough space to work on anything because the playground would be full of kids. But it also meant the entire fourth grade would literally be watching every move he made.

I got outside early to keep an eye on everything. Veena arrived a few minutes later. I think she still felt guilty about revealing Joey's secret, even though his star had been a big hit.

"I don't know what I was thinking," she kept repeating.

I kept saying, "It's fine. Seriously, it's *fine*. Joey loved the attention."

(Kind of a lie since he'd been upset at first. But Veena didn't need to know that.)

Surprisingly, nobody seemed to notice Joey when he wandered outside at the beginning of recess. No heads turned. Nobody spoke to him. Everybody kept hanging out in their own little groups. A bunch of boys kicked a soccer ball back and forth between the swings, making up their own game. Another group bounced a tennis ball off the outside wall of the gym.

Keeping his eyes focused on the ground, Joey didn't seem to notice (or care) that his space was more crowded than usual. Without looking up, he wove around the various groups like a psychic fish moving through a pond.

I heard a couple of kids point out his clothes. His Crocs. The SpongeBob T-shirt under his coat. The short sweat pants with elastic cuffs that bunched above his ankles.

"What's up with your pants, dude?" someone shouted. A few kids behind me snickered.

I turned around to give them a long stare, and they shut up.

Ignoring Veena and me, Joey ambled right past the Buddy Bench. He stopped near the jungle gym in the corner of the playground and studied the compass around his neck for a few seconds. I could hear the whispers circulating among the groups: "What's that gold thing?" "Is he going to make something or not?" "What do you think he'll make?" "Has he started yet?" "What do you think he's doing?"

From somewhere in the middle of the playground, somebody suddenly shouted, "Hey, Joey! Make a tiger!"

Veena's eyes darted toward me, looking surprised. I grinned and shook my head. It was as if some random cosmic pieces just happened to come together at the right time. Spirit Day. Joey. Tiger.

Slowly, the fourth graders picked up the idea and turned it into a chant.

"Ti-ger! Ti-ger!"

Joey's eyes flickered once . . . twice . . . toward the crowd of kids closest to him. I could tell the noise of the chant wasn't making him happy. Holding my breath, I waited for his body to begin its slow slide toward the ground.

But it didn't.

Instead, Joey glanced at the gold disk around his neck again. Then he rummaged around in his coat pocket and eventually pulled out a red plastic soda cap, which he held up for everybody to see. The crowd of fourth graders on the playground grew quiet.

"It's a nose," he announced to the group.

"It's a nose," everybody repeated, echoing him perfectly.

My scalp tingled. Was this really happening?

After dropping the cap on the ground, Joey moved about twenty or thirty feet away from it. Kids backed up to give him enough space to work.

"And this is a tiger," he said, as he began to make a wavy circle—just like the larger one we'd seen from the rooftop with Mr. Ulysses.

"And this is a tiger," the kids repeated.

After that, Joey never looked up again—just kept working with his lips pressed together and his hands clenched into tight fists at his sides.

The fourth graders started chanting "tiger" again, but the chant grew softer as Joey kept going. I have to give the kids credit, though: they kept it up the entire time.

Once or twice, I glanced up to see if Mr. Ulysses was on the school roof, absorbing the great scene, but I never spotted him.

I wish he had been there because there was one moment that felt almost perfect. The sun came out from behind the clouds and shone on the leaves of the 2003 Tree, turning them golden yellow. At the same time, everybody was chanting together, and Joey's shuffling footsteps seemed to match the chant. In that moment, it felt as if all of us—the sporty boys, the popular girls, the bracelet makers, the Pokémon players, Mrs. Zeff, Veena, and me—were helping Joey bring the tiger to life somehow.

Ten minutes later, it was finished.

Joey stopped and shoved his hands into his coat pockets. "Okay, I'm done," he said loudly.

Everyone burst into spontaneous applause.

Veena pulled out her phone. "I want to take a picture of it so I can show my family," she said.

Kids took turns climbing up on the jungle gym and the slide (and anything else they could find) to get a better look at the tiger face. Joey stood off to one side, twisting and untwisting the strand of yarn that held the compass around his neck. A couple of the kids asked him to take their picture next to the tiger. He smiled nervously but said okay.

Although the tiger was much smaller than the one we'd seen from the rooftop with Mr. Ulysses—mostly because the playground was too full of kids this time—it was still pretty impressive.

Before recess ended, Mrs. Zeff texted Mr. Dunner

about bringing the big ladder from the gym so he could take a photo from above to share with the rest of the school. (I know Mr. Ulysses could have done a much better job from the rooftop, but Mrs. Zeff didn't ask us for our opinion.)

Of course, the gym teacher had to make a big production out of carrying the ladder outside, setting it up, and climbing the rungs. He had all the kids chant for him. "Dunner. Dunner. Dunner."

When he got to the top, he gestured at Joey's tiger and yelled, "Okay, so who did all this lousy graffiti all over the playground? They're in real big trouble with me."

Joey didn't get the joke at all. His face froze like a mask, and I was seriously worried he was going to start crying.

But then the gym teacher pointed at Joey and said, "Hey, I'm just joking around with you, kiddo. Isn't this an awesome display of Tiger spirit? Everybody give a big round of applause for Joey Byrd."

The fourth graders clapped and whistled, and Joey's face relaxed a little.

"Who knew we had a famous artist hiding in our school?" the gym teacher continued from his aluminum perch. "I'm gonna send this straight to Cereal News"—which is what everybody jokingly called our local television news station. Tugging a phone out of his back pocket, the gym teacher took a bunch of photos.

And that was the beginning of a month of surprises that no one in Marshallville, Michigan, would ever forget.

April: Cereal News

The following week, you couldn't go anywhere in Marshallville without hearing (or reading) about Joey Byrd. He was a major celebrity. On Tuesday, one of Mr. Dunner's pictures appeared on the front page of the *Marshallville Times* with the headline: "Fourth Grader Brings Tiger Spirit to School Playground." Parents and grandparents all over town shared it on their Facebook pages. The article got thousands of likes.

On Wednesday, a reporter from Cereal News showed up to interview Joey during recess. Although the segment about Joey ended up being only about sixty seconds long—and most of it featured Ms. Getzhammer talking about school pride and community spirit—the story was picked up by one of the network TV stations in Detroit.

They sent a satellite truck and a reporter to film another story about Joey. I had a dentist appointment on the day they came, which was really annoying, but Veena got to be in the background. She was part of a group of kids who pretended to be watching as Joey made a tracing for the news reporter.

In the broadcast, the reporter started out by saying,

"I've heard you can draw anything on the playground, Joey. Is that true?"

Joey shrugged and didn't look at the camera.

"How about Michigan? Can you draw our entire state?" She held her microphone toward Joey with one hand while trying to hold down her windblown hair with the other. "That's a tall order for a fourth grader, isn't it?"

Then Joey replied, "No, not really."

Which totally cracked me up when I watched it that night.

A few seconds later (in TV time), the giant mitten outline of Lower Michigan had appeared, as if by magic, in the middle of the playground. The reporter stood with Joey in the spot where Marshallville was located and waved at the cameraman, who must have been on the roof of our school.

"So that's a bird's-eye view of Michigan from our own Picasso of the playground, Joey Byrd!"

After a brief hesitation, Joey waved too.

April: Outlines

Following the news broadcasts, things began to change even more for Joey. And for us.

In the hallways, Joey still stopped traffic—but in a good way. Younger kids wanted to wave at him. Boys in the older grades greeted him with high fives and "Hey, dude" when they saw him. Kindergarten kids pointed out his classroom on their way to specials and whispered reverently, "That's Joey's room. He does big art." Some teachers started affectionately calling him Picasso.

As each day passed, I swear Joey looked happier and more permanent. It was almost as if his outlines were getting bolder and more filled in. His clothes fit better. His hair was combed. His fists unclenched. He stood up taller, straighter.

My Advice Box got a lot more popular too.

I started getting all kinds of questions about Joey, like how to get his autograph and suggestions for what he should draw next. Some kids sent me their own drawings with notes like: "Do you think I can be a famous artist?"

After I wrote about Joey's spiral of sadness for my October advice column, I got a ton of spiral drawings with more serious questions, such as: "I'm a lot like Joey—how do I make friends?" "What should I do about bullies?" "How can I stop being lonely?"

I had no idea how to choose which ones to answer in the newspaper, so I ended up writing individual notes back to a lot of kids with my advice—decorated with sparkly stickers. Sometimes Veena would help me out.

I'll admit that it was a lot of pressure to write replies to every question I got, but I think it helped some kids feel like *someone* was listening to them, at least. And—let's put it this way—it felt a lot better than just focusing on grades, which used to be the only thing I cared about in school. It also meant that I got a few Bs and one C on an assignment that I completely forgot about because I was so focused on everything else.

Joey's popularity also seemed to pull other forgotten kids out of the shadows. It was as if he shone a bright light on anyone who was hiding in a corner or standing against a wall alone. The outcasts started getting noticed. The excluded were included.

Veena and I witnessed this firsthand.

One recess, a couple of the sporty kids walked over to the boys in the Pokémon group and invited them to play soccer. We were shocked to see the boys leave their precious boxes of cards behind as they galloped eagerly toward the fields with their new friends.

Another day, the bracelet-making girls added someone new to their group—a shy, stringy-haired girl named

Margaret who usually sat by herself on the swings with a stuffed unicorn. At some point, the unicorn got its own beaded necklace.

In sixth grade, Wally Rensbacher suddenly became a topic of conversation.

I overheard a couple of boys asking him questions about Asperger's syndrome. They wanted to know what it was and how it felt to have it. A petition for hosting a special contest for Wally was circulated around the sixth grade. It would be a Presidential Quiz Competition, so Wally could test his skills against other schools and find more kids who liked presidents as much as he did.

What made me really happy was the fact that the petition wasn't even my idea. A group of boys and Wally started it. Our social studies teacher agreed to be the competition's advisor.

In the meantime, Joey's designs kept getting better and better. Every recess, he seemed to come up with something more spectacular than the day before. There was no way of guessing what might appear next in the wood chips.

A superhero could emerge. Or a dragon spouting fire. Or Ms. Getzhammer's cat—yes, she actually asked him to draw her cat. Or a college basketball or football logo. (Sports seemed to be a frequent theme, and I had a feeling the boys in Joey's class had something to do with that.)

Another recess, Veena showed Joey some of the geometric art made with colored powder in India. They are called *rangoli* designs and they are created on the floor outside a doorway or hall for special occasions. "Maybe you could try something like this someday," she told him.

A few days later, he made one that looked like a giant sunburst for her. I honestly thought Veena was going to cry when she saw it.

My all-time favorite Joey creation was Yoda with the Tree Ear. One afternoon at recess, Joey did a huge outline of Yoda from *Star Wars*—only he drew it with the 2003 Tree growing out of Yoda's left ear. It was a huge hit. I don't know where Joey got the idea, but the 2003 Tree became known as the Yoda Tree from that day on.

JOEYBYRD

Drawing Yoda with a tree in his ear was Joey's idea. His teacher was reading a book called *The Strange Case of Origami Yoda* to his class. It was a very funny story, and Joey really liked it. It was the first book he'd ever liked—partly because it made him laugh and partly because he didn't have to read it himself.

In science, they were learning about trees.

Somehow, the two ideas came together in his brain.

Trees. Funny Yoda.

Luckily, there was a tree on Marshallville's playground already.

All he had to do was draw Yoda around it.

April: Firsts

Joey wasn't the only source of surprise and wonder. During the second week of October, two more things occurred that were both surprising and unexpected.

The first one happened to me.

Someone put a note in my Advice Box sometime between Tuesday and Thursday morning when I checked the box. The note was written in blue ink on notebook paper—and I thought the handwriting kind of looked like a boy's writing because of the small, squarish printing.

It said: *Dear April, I am a sixth grader who admires you greatly, and I hope that one day we can be friends. Sincerely yours, Anonamous*

Although Anonymous was spelled wrong, I was convinced the letter wasn't a joke. The handwriting looked too neat. And nobody would write something as polite and formal as *I'm a sixth grader who admires you greatly* if they were joking.

But who had written it?

(Okay, I will admit that part of me hoped it was Tanner Torchman—although I knew that was crazy. He had plenty of friends *and* a girlfriend.)

So, who had left it? I wondered if it could have come from someone in one of my classes. Or Wally Rensbacher, perhaps?

Then we got our next surprise: a freak snowstorm on October 10.

Of course, nobody was prepared. We were only supposed to get a few flakes, but then a couple inches of snow fell overnight. We woke up to everything being covered in a beautiful blanket of white. A lot of kids thought it should have been a snow day, but it wasn't.

That morning, Ms. Getzhammer called for indoor recess because so many kids weren't dressed for the weather. "Tell your parents to dig out those gloves and hats and coats for you," she said during morning announcements. "Tomorrow I'll be sending everyone outdoors, no matter what. No excuses. Be prepared."

Sometime during lunch or indoor recess, Joey managed to slip outside without being noticed. I have a sneaking suspicion Mr. Ulysses may have helped him. I saw the janitor carrying around his Polaroid camera and—oddly—a pair of kid-sized snow boots.

Word spread quickly after lunch.

Three giant snowflakes had appeared in the snow on our playground.

JOEYBYRD

Joey had never made his tracings in the playground snow before. Usually he didn't get outside until after the snow was already trampled.

Now it stretched in front of him like a smooth sheet of white frosting.

It was Mr. Ulysses's idea to make the snowflakes and surprise everyone. Joey wasn't sure he liked working in the snow. Everything on the playground seemed different than what he was used to. The Buddy Bench had turned from blue to white. The tree looked as if it was covered in wet cotton balls. The boots that Mr. Ulysses had found for him felt weird. They were too big. But the janitor told Joey that he couldn't wear his Crocs. It was too cold.

Joey found it was harder to hide his mistakes. When he messed up, he couldn't smooth away the extra footprints in the snow. He made a couple of mistakes. And a lot of his lines were really crooked because of the stupid boots.

Mr. Ulysses said that was okay, because nothing in nature was perfect. Not even snowflakes.

April: Nothing Is Perfect

I suppose it was inevitable that there would be problems for Joey. And for us. Things couldn't be perfect one hundred percent of the time. People weren't perfect. Life wasn't perfect.

Eventually, a bunch of the Pokémon boys quit the soccer team and went back to their cards . . . they said soccer was boring but they were still going to be friends with everyone.

Then the girl with the stuffed unicorn got mad at the bracelet group and returned to her old spot.

I didn't get any more notes from my mystery admirer either. I began to think that maybe it was a joke after all. Finally, I shoved the note into the back of my locker and vowed to stop stressing about it.

Problems started to crop up with Joey too.

One recess—I think it was a week or so after the snowstorm—Veena and I were sitting on the Buddy Bench when Joey wandered outside, looking upset. I noticed that his coat pockets seemed to be stuffed with something. What was he bringing outside? I wondered.

As he walked closer, a few scraps of paper fell out of his pockets and scattered behind him like bread crumbs. Joey didn't seem to realize anything was wrong.

"Joey, hey, wait up! You're dropping stuff all over the place." I jumped up from the bench and tried to get his attention. Veena followed me.

Stopping in his tracks, Joey looked over his shoulder blankly. Veena and I scurried to pick up the scraps that were within reach. Then I caught the writing on one of them. It said: *PLEASE, Joey! Make a picture of a football and a soccer ball for my birthday!* Another had hearts and rainbows around the edges. It said: *You are my BEST best friend! Can you draw a picture for me with my name on it?* Another folded message had a dollar bill taped to it.

My heart sunk. We should have realized this would happen, right? It was inevitable that things would start to spin out of control eventually. The more Joey did for people, the more requests he got. And I was probably as guilty of encouraging it as anyone else.

I caught Veena's worried look as she returned with more notes in her hands. Clearly, she'd figured out what was going on as quickly as I did.

"What should we do?" she whispered.

"I'm not sure."

I tried to read Joey's expression. Was he upset by all the requests? Or confused by them? Or was he just feeling overwhelmed?

As usual, his face gave nothing away.

"Are these notes from kids in your class?" I finally asked, trying not to sound concerned or panicked.

"Yes," he mumbled, staring at his feet—which were in sneakers today. "And other kids too," he added softly.

"From other grades?"

Joey kept looking down. "Everyone."

I didn't want to wreck Joey's popularity or make him mad at us, but it was obvious that something needed to be done.

"Okay," I said, trying to make eye contact with him. "I know you want to be nice, but you don't have to make tracings for anyone else unless you want to. If you don't want to make something, you just tell people that you do your own designs. It is your art. Or you can send them over to us and we'll tell them for you."

Veena nodded, but Joey was silent. He stared at his shoes. I couldn't tell if he was listening or not.

"Seriously, Joey"—I made my voice more firm—"you are the artist and you get to make your own decisions. Nobody can force you to do their ideas. Repeat after me: I'm the artist and no one can tell me what art to make."

Very reluctantly, Joey repeated the words. "I'm the artist and no one can tell me what art to make."

I gave him an encouraging smile. "Good. I know you can do it."

"Do you want me to take all of your notes and throw them away for you?" Veena asked.

Finally, Joey's face broke into a smile. "Okay," he said.

Then he began pulling fistfuls of paper—notebook paper, colored construction paper, crayon hearts, folded paper footballs—out of his pockets and pushing them into Veena's hands. She shoved them into her own coat pockets as fast as he emptied his. More scraps drifted to the ground, and I picked them up.

From what I could tell, most of them had never been opened.

Once his pockets were totally empty, Joey's face relaxed. His shoulders rose as if we'd just taken a big weight off of them.

"Any more?" I asked, just to be sure.

"Nope." Joey smiled. "I'm good."

"Remember: you are the artist and nobody can tell you what to make," I called out again as Joey shuffled away from us in his usual way.

The next day, he did a beautiful unicorn galloping across the playground.

Margaret, the stringy-haired girl who was obsessed with unicorns, loved it so much that Ms. Getzhammer had to come outside to coax her off the playground at the end of recess.

The following day, Joey did a giant Pikachu.

President Lincoln also appeared on our playground one afternoon. It took everyone a while to figure that one out. Joey drew him in profile like he is pictured on the penny. Wally Rensbacher talked about it for days afterward.

Was it a coincidence that Joey's new creations matched the interests of some of the outcast kids? Was he taking my advice and doing what he wanted to do now?

It was impossible to tell for sure, although Veena and I both thought he seemed a lot happier.

But then, Joey received the biggest request of his life, and my advice would definitely play a part in what happened next.

April: Invitation

At the end of October, there were two big nights in Marshallville. Halloween was always popular—like it is everywhere else. Homecoming was the other major event.

If the weather was nice, half the town would show up for Marshallville's Homecoming game. The high school went all out for it. There would be floats and fireworks. The high school marching band always did a special pre-game show. Often the mayor and his family dressed up in rented tiger costumes and handed out candy to the crowd. Most of the stores and restaurants in town offered special discounts for the weekend. Sometimes there were carnival rides in the high school parking lot.

Despite the popularity of Homecoming, it never occurred to me that Joey Byrd would be asked to be part of the festivities. Like I said, it was a high school event. It had its own longstanding traditions and routines. Younger kids generally weren't part of the show—unless you were one of the mayor's three blond-haired kids.

When Mr. Mac called Veena and me to his office during Friday's recess (a week before Homecoming), we had no idea why. All Mrs. Zeff told us was that he wanted to talk to us about something.

After we sat down, the counselor told us he had good news to share—which was a relief since we thought something was wrong.

"I just got off the phone with the principal of the high school," Mr. Mac said with a big grin. "And it's really fantastic news"—he paused for dramatic effect. "The high school has invited Joey to be part of the big Homecoming game against the Kenston Eagles next week. They want him to draw a giant tiger on the football field as a surprise during the pregame show." Leaning back in his chair, Mr. Mac looked at us. "So what do you think?"

It took me a minute to absorb what the counselor was actually saying.

They wanted Joey to make a tiger for Homecoming? On the huge football field at the high school? With his *feet*?

Veena glanced uncertainly at me. I could tell she was totally confused by the whole conversation. I'm guessing they probably didn't have anything like Homecoming in India.

"How exactly would he draw on the field?" I asked, trying to keep my voice from sounding as if I thought Mr. Mac was completely nuts.

The counselor smiled. "You know, I had the exact same question. How would Joey draw on a football field? But the high school grounds crew had a fantastic idea. They thought Joey could use a chalk spreader—you know, the kind of thing they use for lining baseball diamonds—and he could make a giant tiger on the grass right before the start of the game. You know—with chalk instead of his feet." Mr. Mac squiggled an invisible line on the table in front of us to demonstrate.

He continued, "Of course, the picture wouldn't last very long. Only a couple of minutes probably. Once the football players ran onto the field, that's it"—he swept his hands through the air. "The art would be gone. But imagine how cool it would be! Marshallville would have something at its Homecoming that no other high school in history has ever done—well, as far as we know."

He leaned forward and lowered his voice. "Also, we could use a little extra luck this year because the Eagles have a much better team than us. So . . . what do you think of the idea, ladies?"

I was still having trouble grasping the whole concept. "You mean . . . he would draw the chalk tiger *in front of* the crowd at Homecoming?"

"Yep." The counselor nodded and smiled. "Pretty neat, huh?" Then his face grew more serious. "So, you both know Joey best—do you think he'd do it?"

No, I thought, there was *no way* he'd do it.

The truth was *I* wouldn't do it. Not for a million dollars. Perform in front of hundreds of screaming high schoolers? At the biggest game of the year? Against our biggest rivals? Just the thought of it made my stomach churn.

I shook my head. "No, I don't think he would."

Although Joey had changed a lot since he'd become famous, he hadn't completely transformed into a regular kid. Every recess, he still went straight to the most deserted spots on the playground to work by himself. We still had to keep an eye on him to make sure other kids didn't overwhelm him. And even though he didn't lie down in the hallways anymore, his body still jerked back whenever people got too close or too loud.

Next to me, Veena agreed. "He is very shy."

But Mr. Mac ignored us completely. "Well, I think there's no harm in asking Joey about it," he continued. "Let's see what he says." Spinning around in his chair, the counselor reached for the phone on his desk. "Who knows? Maybe he'll surprise us." He called the front office and asked them to send Joey in from recess.

About five minutes later, there was an almost inaudible tap on the counselor's door.

"Come in!" Mr. Mac called out.

Joey opened the door just a crack and squeezed through the narrow opening in his usual way. His cheeks were scarlet from the cold. His hair stuck up in weedy, windblown clumps. He sat down tentatively, as if the chair might explode beneath him.

"Good gracious, you look like a block of ice, Joey," Mr. Mac remarked.

"I'm fine," Joey insisted. His eyes strayed to the window behind Mr. Mac. I could tell he wanted to be back outside. He never liked to be interrupted when he was working.

"Okay, well, this won't take long. You're not in trouble or anything, so you can relax." Mr. Mac smiled one of his goofy smiles. "We just called you here to my office because we have an interesting proposal for you to consider. . . ."

At that point, I figured that Joey had probably tuned out altogether. An interesting proposal? Who did the counselor think he was talking to?

But as Mr. Mac continued, I noticed how Joey's eyes suddenly shifted to the counselor's face. When Mr. Mac started explaining about the football field and about drawing a big tiger in chalk for the game against the Eagles, Joey seemed to be hanging on to every word.

"So what do you think, kiddo?" Mr. Mac sat back and folded his arms over the Mickey Mouse tie he was wearing. "You want to give this a try or not?"

"You mean the football field by the big high school?" Joey repeated. "That's the field where I would draw?"

Mr. Mac nodded. "Yes, you could use as much—or as little—of the space as you wanted to—"

"But a ton of people will be there," I blurted out, trying to make Joey realize that this was an *extremely bad idea*. "It's the Kenston Eagles versus the Marshallville Tigers. If you've never been to a Homecoming game before, trust me—it's a huge game."

I may not have been a big fan of football, but even I knew about the Kenston rivalry. It had been going on for years and years. Kenston was on the other side of Battle Creek, so they were a cereal town too.

I tried to get Joey to see how it was one thing to make a tiger on the playground with a bunch of fourth graders watching, but it was another thing entirely to draw on an enormous football field *by yourself* in front of stands packed with hundreds of rowdy, out-of-control high schoolers. "Everybody will be really loud and crazy," I said.

"I'm sure it will be a lot of pressure," Veena added.

But our non-subtle hints didn't seem to get through to Joey.

I could almost see the little wheels turning in his brain. I could tell that he was only thinking about that gigantic expanse of green stretching from end zone to end zone. I knew he was picturing the biggest tiger he'd ever made—on the biggest, greenest playground around.

Joey scooted up a little straighter in his chair.

"Okay," he agreed with an excited smile. "Yes."

JOEYBYRD

Actually, Joey didn't care at all about the tiger. Or about Marshallville vs. Kenston. Or Homecoming. Or football.

All he heard was the word "eagle." All he could picture was *Aquila audax*. His favorite bird.

That's why he said yes.

April: The Art Machine

I thought Mr. Ulysses would be as concerned as we were about Joey and Homecoming, but he wasn't.

After leaving the counselor's office, Veena and I went in search of the janitor, hoping he'd know what to do next. We found him in the intermediate hallway, fixing a broken locker.

Once I finished telling him what had happened, he seemed as excited by the idea as Mr. Mac had been.

His eyes lit up. "I know exactly how to make that chalk machine for Joey," he said. Plucking a used envelope and a pencil from his shirt pocket, he began to sketch something on the back of the envelope. For a couple of minutes, he seemed to forget we were there.

After he finished, Mr. Ulysses showed us his drawing. "How's this?" He pointed at something that looked like a cross between a lawn mower and a kid's wagon. "See, I'd take the chalk spreader and I'd add some extra parts to make it work better for Joey and give it more style. Special handles. A larger tank. A fancy funnel for pouring in extra chalk if he needs it." He pointed at more marks I could barely see.

Finally, I had to point-blank ask, "So do you think it's okay?"

Still preoccupied with his design, Mr. Ulysses glanced up. "Is what okay?"

I held back a sigh. "For Joey to draw a tiger on the field for Homecoming?"

"Didn't you already say he'd agree to do it?" Mr. Ulysses's forehead scrunched with confusion. He glanced back and forth at Veena and me.

"Yes," we answered reluctantly.

The janitor smiled and shrugged. "Then I don't see what the problem is. I think it's a wonderful opportunity for Joey. Especially if he's excited about it. Who knows where it could lead in the future?" he said, echoing what he'd told me weeks before.

The greatest things often start with a simple line.

He reached into his back pocket for a phone. "In fact, I'm gonna call up my buddies at the high school right now and tell them I'd be glad to build that chalk machine for Joey. It'll be my contribution to the cause," he added.

Mr. Ulysses built the entire machine over the weekend.

On Monday, he pushed it outside during the fourth-grade recess to show it off. I didn't realize what it was at first.

It looked like a bizarre musical instrument on wheels.

Sunlight glinted off a brass funnel from a trumpet (or a trombone?) on the top. Below the funnel, there was a large orange tank where I assumed the chalk was stored. Handlebars were attached to each side of the tank for pushing the machine. The four sturdy wheels below the tank looked as if they might have come from a child's wagon.

The chalk machine was an instant attraction. After Mr. Ulysses got it outside, half of the recess kids came running over to see what it was. Joey wandered over too.

The janitor called it Joey's Art Machine. "This is what Joey is going to use at the Homecoming football game on Friday to make a big design on the field," he explained.

"Joey's going to be at Homecoming?" someone blurted out because nothing had been announced yet.

The janitor grinned at Joey. "Yep."

The whole group burst into applause. I knew it wouldn't be long before the news had spread to the rest of the school.

Mr. Ulysses waved Joey forward. "Okay, come on over here, Joey. Let's see how well this thing works."

The crowd parted to let Joey slip through. He looked both enthralled with the machine—and terrified of it, at the same time.

"First, the chalk goes into this fancy brass funnel and it's stored in this big tank below." Mr. Ulysses tapped the orange tank. "To spread the chalk, you just push the machine like a lawn mower." He demonstrated pushing the chalk spreader back and forth. "And this handle makes the line start and stop when you press it." The janitor squeezed a silver handle that looked as if it was an old bicycle brake. The chalk line stopped.

He pushed the machine toward Joey. "Now, you try it, kiddo."

Clenching his lips together, Joey gingerly placed his hands on the metal handlebars.

"Go ahead—give it a try." Mr. Ulysses smiled encouragingly. "You can do it."

After he pushed the machine forward and a bright line of white chalk appeared on the ground behind him, Joey's face relaxed.

He made a circle. Then a squiggle. Then a smile flitted across his face as he drew a big letter M for Marshallville.

The fourth graders clapped. He gave a small bow—which was something I'd never seen him do before. Other kids lined up to try out the machine. Pretty soon, the wood chips on our part of the playground had turned totally white.

Of course, the fourth graders couldn't resist stamping their feet in the chalk. Somehow the powder ended up getting tossed in the air too. Clouds of chalk dust drifted around us. Kids laughed and danced in the sparkly-white air. It was one of those moments I'll always remember from elementary school—seeing the fourth graders having so much fun dancing and spinning in the chalk-dust clouds.

I remember hearing one of the fourth-grade girls tell Mr. Ulysses, "You know, you should invent a lot more stuff. This is so fun."

"You think so?" Mr. Ulysses replied, looking both surprised and proud.

"Yeah, this is really cool." A bunch of the kids who were standing nearby nodded. "You should definitely make more things."

"Maybe I will." Mr. Ulysses gave a knowing smile. "Maybe I will."

April: The Invisible Feeling of Wings

As Homecoming approached, the surprises continued.

On Wednesday, I was getting my books out of my locker during the usual chaos that happens in the morning before school starts, when a boy's voice said, "Hey, April."

My heart jumped. I turned around cautiously to see who had said my name. Tanner's friend Jacob and another boy named Noah Langley stood behind me with their backpacks slung loosely over their shoulders.

I knew Jacob because he was in most of my classes.

Noah was in my language arts class and homeroom, but I'd never talked to him that much. Like Jacob, he usually hung out with Tanner's group. I'd heard some of the girls refer to him as Noah the Nose because he had a largish nose, although I didn't think it was that noticeable. Unlike a lot of the boys in sixth grade, Noah was pretty quiet and he tended to wear hiker-type T-shirts and jeans instead of the usual Nike gear.

"So, we were just wondering . . . are you going to the Homecoming game on Friday or not?" Jacob asked me loudly, while glancing sideways at Noah and smirking.

"Why?" I replied cautiously.

Although I was planning to help out with Joey at the

pregame show, I wasn't sure it was a good idea to reveal that information to Jacob. I couldn't tell if his question was a setup or not. Sometimes he could take jokes too far.

Jacob smirked more. Noah seemed to be concentrating on something on his phone. "Because Noah wants to know." He poked Noah with an elbow. "Don't you, dude?"

Blushing furiously, Noah looked up from his phone and glared at Jacob. "No I don't. Just shut up, okay?" He gave Jacob a half-hearted shove.

Grinning, Jacob shoved back. "Don't lie, dude. Remember that letter you gave her?"

What? My brain tried to catch up with what I'd just heard.

"Shut the heck up." Noah rammed his shoulder into Jacob.

"Hey, you know you like her." Jacob returned the shove.

Then Noah's heavy backpack started sliding off his shoulder, and he had to kind of catch the backpack and not drop his phone and not fall into me, all at the same time. Meanwhile, my head was spinning because I was still thinking about Jacob's comment. Was he saying that Noah Langley was the one who had written the great-admirer letter to me?

Anyway, there was this awkward, unbalanced moment when everything seemed to be sliding or falling. And my body was kind of frozen and my brain was trying to catch up. I remember reaching my hand out to keep Noah's phone (or him) from falling, and I think I said, "Whoa," which was a totally stupid thing to say, but that's what I said.

But here's the thing—as Noah caught his backpack and straightened up, he smiled at me for one millisecond. (Like if you blinked, you would have missed it.) And I think Jacob must have blinked, because I don't think he saw it.

Still, I could tell, just from that one millisecond smile, that Noah Langley liked me.

And I was one hundred percent sure he'd written the letter.

"So are you coming to the game or not?" Jacob asked in a rush, as Noah yanked his backpack onto his shoulder and took off down the hall.

"Yeah, I'm pretty sure I'm going," I said in this casual voice, even though I already knew I would definitely be there for the pregame show, along with Veena, Mr. Mac, and Mr. Ulysses.

Why did I give such a vague answer?

Maybe I needed time to think. Maybe I didn't want to sound too desperate.

"Great. We'll be in Section E behind the high school band people. Noah will be waiting for you," Jacob yelled over his shoulder as he plunged into the crowd after him.

At that moment, it felt like a thousand wings were fluttering inside me.

JOEYBYRD

That same morning, Joey went on a tour of the high school football field. Even though he usually practiced his tracings in his mind, the high school football coaches wanted him to practice on the field. *Practice makes perfect,* they said.

Joey didn't mind leaving school, because he got to miss a quiz in math.

The coaches who came to pick him up were called Coach Glen and Coach Baker. Coach Glen was thin with a stopwatch around his neck—which Joey liked. It reminded him of his compass. Coach Baker was large and smelled like garlic—which Joey didn't like.

Mr. Ulysses brought over the chalk machine.

When Joey stepped onto the empty football field for the first time, he was surprised by how different it felt from the playground. First of all, it had very bright green grass. It reminded him of Christmas cookie frosting.

Second, it crunched strangely under his feet. He wasn't sure it was real.

The coaches wanted Joey to practice making the tiger with the chalk machine. *To see how it will work,* they said. But Joey ignored them. He started pushing the machine across the crunchy green grass to make the scalloped feathers of an enormous eagle's wing.

Although Joey couldn't hear their conversation, this is what the coaches said after a few minutes of watching him from the empty stands:

Coach Baker leaned toward Coach Glenn and said under his breath, "That look like a tiger to you?"

Coach Glenn mumbled that he wasn't exactly sure.

"It looks like a wing to me. What kind of tiger has wings?" Coach Baker said. He turned toward Mr. Ulysses, who was standing on the other side of him. "Do you know what in the heck the little kid is making?"

"If I were making a guess," Mr. Ulysses said slowly, "I'd say it might be a bird—possibly an eagle."

That's when Coach Baker blew his whistle and hollered at Joey to Stop. Right. There. He ran down the bleacher steps and jogged onto the field.

"What in the heck are you doing, kid?" he yelled at Joey, and waved his arms. "We've already got enough trouble this season. We don't need a jinx, kid!"

Joey had been called a lot of names in life, but he had never been called a jinx before.

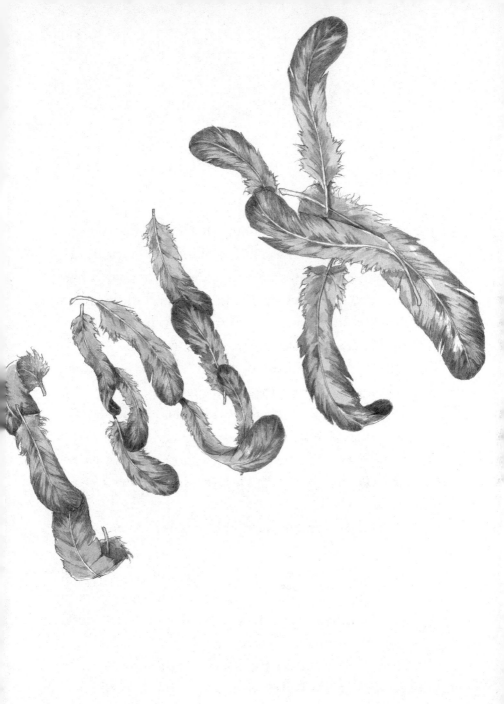

April: Choosing Sides

I was so lost in thinking about what had happened with Noah and Jacob in the hallway before school started—replaying it a million times in my head to remember exactly what was said and who said it—that I didn't notice the fact that Joey was upset at recess. Veena was the one who had to point it out to me.

"Look at what Joey's doing today," she said in an urgent voice, bumping my arm to get my attention.

When I looked toward the swing sets, I could see right away what she meant. The lines uncoiled from Joey's feet in a tight spiral. His hands were clenched at his sides and his face was tense and pale. He was ignoring everyone and everything as he walked.

"Should we go over and talk to him?" Veena asked, looking worried.

Although I didn't want anything to ruin my floaty feeling of happiness, I could see that something was wrong with Joey. Really wrong. He hadn't made a spiral in weeks.

"I guess we should," I said with a sigh.

Getting up from the Buddy Bench, we walked across the playground. When we got close to Joey, I called out,

"Hey, Veena and I noticed that you seemed kind of upset today. Is something bothering you?"

Joey stopped and stared past us. "No," he said to the air molecules. "I'm fine."

I glanced at Veena. Why was he acting so oddly? "Well, that doesn't sound very convincing," I replied.

Then Veena added, "Did something happen in your classroom today?"

"No," Joey said. His mouth tightened into a line. Under his breath, he added, "I wasn't in my room today."

"Okay . . . ," Veena asked, "where were you?"

"I was on the football field practicing." Joey waved his arm vaguely in the direction of the high school. "But I'm NOT making a tiger," he blurted out fiercely.

Veena gave me a confused look. I had no idea what Joey was talking about either. How could he have been on the high school football field during school? What did he mean about not making a tiger? Was he trying to tell us he wanted to quit Homecoming?

"Why can't you make a tiger?" I asked carefully.

Joey gave the wood chips a hard kick with one sneaker, sending bits of bark flying. "BECAUSE I DON'T WANT TO MAKE ONE!" he yelled at me.

Veena and I both took a step back, pretty shocked. We'd never seen Joey yell at anything before. Tears welled up in his eyes and started flowing in bright, shiny streaks down his cheeks.

Looking stricken, Veena rushed toward Joey and gave

him a quick hug. "It's okay," she said, patting his shoulder lightly with her hand after she stepped back. "No matter what happened, we will help you."

At least Joey didn't shove her away.

After giving Joey a couple of seconds to calm down, I tried again. "When you said you don't want to make a tiger, do you mean you don't want to be part of Homecoming anymore—that you want to quit?"

"No," Joey replied, glaring at me through his tears. "I'm not making a tiger because I don't want to. I'm making an eagle instead. It's the best bird ever. I already have everything planned right here." He jabbed a finger toward his head. "It is going to be my best tracing ever. I don't need help from anybody. I already know what I'm doing."

"Ahhh," I exhaled. Now the problem was becoming clear.

Joey wanted to draw an eagle because it was his favorite bird, I guessed. Maybe he pictured himself being like an eagle—or maybe he just liked eagles in general. Who knows?

However, our biggest rivals were the Eagles. We had been rivals for years. For obvious reasons, he couldn't draw an eagle at our Homecoming game.

It was Tigers vs. Eagles. Only in art instead of football.

I scrambled to come up with an easy solution.

"How about this idea? Maybe you could use this week's game to *practice* what it's like to draw on a big field," I suggested. "Since you've already done a tiger and you're really good at it, you could draw a tiger this week. Then you could draw something more elaborate for the next game, like a big eagle, and impress everyone."

Joey's expression didn't change.

So I tried explaining more about Homecoming—how it was the day when people who grew up in Marshallville would come back to root for their home team. "It's a big honor to be part of it. And you're a Tiger because you live here in Marshallville. It's your home team. You can't draw an eagle, because that's the mascot of the other side."

Joey kicked the dirt. "No, I'm on both sides," he insisted.

I told him that was kind of impossible—that the point of a sport was choosing a side to be on . . . to root for. "You know, the other side is like the enemy," I said.

"I know. That's why I invented my own sport at recess," Joey insisted. His voice rose higher, and he seemed to be on the verge of crying again. "Because it doesn't have sides. It's just making tracings."

I was starting to feel like pulling my hair out. "But people will *think* you're cheering for the other side if you make an eagle, because that's their mascot."

"But I'm not cheering. I'm making my tracings," Joey retorted.

I sighed loudly and looked over at Veena, who was shaking her head. Joey kept kicking the ground. We were getting nowhere. I was losing my patience.

"Look," I said finally. "If you make an eagle, *nobody* is

going to understand it. Everybody in our stands will boo and yell. The high school kids will probably throw things onto the field and mess up your tracing and be really rude. And you'll get called a traitor and probably a bunch of other bad things. You don't want that to happen, do you?"

I knew it was a harsh thing to say, but I didn't know how else to get through to him.

Without saying a word, Joey suddenly bolted toward me. For a half second, I was afraid he was going to plow right into me. But he stopped a few inches short of pushing me over.

"YOU TOLD ME I'M THE ARTIST AND NO-BODY CAN TELL ME WHAT ART TO MAKE!" he shouted in my face. Then he ran toward the back doors of the school and disappeared inside.

April: The Coat

I was convinced Joey would quit.

After the scene on the playground, I couldn't sleep that night. I felt awful about how I'd yelled at him. It wasn't like me at all. What I should have said was: "Do whatever you want to do at Homecoming—be original, be creative, don't worry about what other people think—make a tiger with purple spots if you want to—draw the biggest, baddest eagle anybody has ever seen—and make it fly over Marshallville—be yourself—"

Why had I gotten so upset with Joey? Was it because he couldn't see things the way everyone else did?

Or was it because I couldn't see things the way he did?

Had I yelled at him because I was frustrated with *myself,* not with him?

That idea made me feel even worse.

I decided to talk to Mr. Mac or Mr. Ulysses first thing in the morning and tell them the whole story. If they thought Joey should pull out of Homecoming—or do something else—then maybe they could figure out how to handle it.

But I couldn't find either of them. Mr. Mac's door was shut and his office was dark. I searched the hallways for

Mr. Ulysses and knocked on the boiler room door twice, but he didn't answer.

I had a math test and a project to work on in language arts that morning, so I couldn't leave to search for them again. Then something else happened with Joey during the fourth-grade lunch.

Lunch had just started when I noticed a bunch of high schoolers walk out of the school office with Ms. Getzhammer and head toward the cafeteria. I was on my way to the library to get some books for my language arts project.

There were two girls in cheerleader outfits and four enormous football players in their Tigers jerseys. They were talking and laughing loudly among themselves and seemed to be pointing out things they remembered in the school.

What was up? I wondered.

I picked up my books and took a detour past the cafeteria. By the time I got there, the entire room was silent and only Ms. Getzhammer was talking. I caught the tail end of her speech. "And now the high school spirit squad has a very special gift to give to Joey for the big game tomorrow night. Come on up here, Joey."

Oh no. My heart started to pound. *What was happening?*

As everybody in the cafeteria clapped, Joey's classmates urged him forward. His face was expressionless as he got up from his lunch table—which I knew was his totally panicked look. He made his way toward the front at the pace of a turtle.

When Joey finally reached the group, Ms. Getzhammer handed the microphone to the largest football player, who was about three times the size of Joey.

"Yeah, hi, everybody—whoa, that's loud," the football player bellowed into the microphone, making the whole room crack up. Joey's face looked more panicked.

The player kept talking. "Well, yeah, uh, I'm Carson Taggert, defensive lineman for the Tigers. And we wanted to bring a gift for Joey because we heard he needed some new spirit gear for the big game tomorrow night. So . . ."

The lineman looked toward one of the cheerleaders, who stepped forward with an orange coat. It was one of the expensive letterman-type coats made of black wool with orange leather sleeves. Usually the high school sports players were the only ones who owned them.

The entire room of fourth graders gasped.

"Go ahead, try it out," the football player said as the cheerleader helped Joey to pull it on.

The coat was so large it could have wrapped around Joey twice. His body seemed to sway under the weight of it.

"Well, I guess it's a *little* big," the football player joked. "But look at what it says on the back."

Joey craned his neck around to see the back, which he couldn't. Finally, the cheerleader turned him around, so all of us could see the white letters ironed on the black wool. They spelled out:

JOEY BYRD, TEAM ARTIST.

"It says Joey Byrd, Team Artist," the football player

announced. "So you're, like, one of our team now. Isn't that cool? Let's everybody give Joey a big round of applause."

I was really surprised when Joey held out his bright orange sleeves and turned around to show off the coat again. The room went crazy.

But I have to admit that there was something about the moment that bothered me too.

As everybody cheered, I could see how easy it would be for Joey Byrd to lose who he was. All it took was a coat to begin to transform him into us. How long would it be before we changed everything about him and he stopped being who he was? What would happen then?

Up front, the high schoolers took turns giving Joey high fives, and then Ms. Getzhammer announced that everybody could go back to eating lunch.

Joey wore his new coat to recess that afternoon—so I guess he must have liked it. I watched him wander around the playground in it, and he even let a couple of kids try it on.

He didn't seem to be upset any longer—not like he'd been the day before. I couldn't decide whether to try talking to him about Homecoming or not. At one point, he flopped down in the middle of the playground for a few minutes and seemed to be thinking about something.

I waited until he sat up again. Then I wandered over to where he was sitting. Crouching down next to him, I said, "Hey, I just wanted to come over and tell you that I'm really sorry about getting mad at you yesterday. I shouldn't have yelled at you like that."

"That's okay," Joey replied, trailing his fingers through the wood chips.

"Are you doing better today?"

Not looking up, Joey nodded. "Yep. I'm good now."

"So are you going to be part of Homecoming tomorrow night?" I casually asked.

Joey nodded. "Yes."

I hesitated a moment before asking, "And did you decide what you're drawing?"

"Yep. I definitely know what I'm doing now," Joey replied in this confident voice. He looked up. "I'm not mad or sad anymore. Everybody will like what I'm doing." Then he smiled and gave me this funny thumbs-up sign. "You will like it too."

Although I was pretty sure his answer meant he was making a tiger—a small part of me still wasn't sure what Joey Byrd might do.

"Okay, well, I can't wait to see it," I said.

"Me too," Joey answered.

April: Dancing on Sunshine

On Homecoming Day, summer returned for one last brief visit. We were lucky. Even though it was almost the end of October, the air was warm. The sky was Buddy Bench blue. And the few leaves that remained on the Yoda Tree were gold.

I wasn't a dancer, but I spun around in place when I got to the Buddy Bench on Friday afternoon. "Isn't this fantastic!" I said to Veena, stretching my arms out in the air.

Veena seemed startled by my exuberance. "Yes," she said with a nervous smile. She twisted her dark hair in her fingers. "I'm looking forward to the Homecoming tonight. I've never been to an American football match before."

"Game. Football *game*," I corrected her.

"Game," she repeated, shaking her head. "I keep mixing up our sport and yours." In India, football meant soccer.

"Trust me, you'll catch on." I grinned.

The one thing I couldn't figure out how to tell Veena was the fact that I probably wouldn't be sitting with her at the game. We had made arrangements to meet each other for the pregame show, of course. Veena's parents were bringing her. My brother was going to drop me off early because my parents had dinner plans. They would bring me home after the game.

But I couldn't bring myself to tell Veena that I'd been invited to sit with Noah and the sixth graders.

Why not? I guess because I figured there was still a chance it might not work out—that maybe I wouldn't be able to find the sixth graders—or maybe I'd lose my nerve and decide not to meet up with Noah after all.

Plus, I couldn't bear to ruin Veena's excitement about Homecoming. We spent most of recess talking about the game. She pestered me with a million questions. What to wear. What to bring. Where to meet. When to cheer. I explained touchdowns and field goals to her three times, because she was really worried about messing up that part. "I don't want to cheer when nobody else is," she said.

We didn't pay much attention to Joey because he seemed happy and focused on making a tracing. From what we could tell, he was covering the playground with one of his wave-like designs. His lines looped and curled through the dirt. They swirled around the swing sets and the jungle gym.

"He looks like he's having fun," Veena commented.

And he was.

Later on, we would figure out what he was trying to tell us.

April: Vanilla Farm

By the time I got home from school on Friday, there wasn't much time to get ready for Homecoming. My bus dropped me off at four, and Luke had to take me to the game at five-thirty.

Being a perfectionist, I spent about a half hour on my hair, getting it perfectly smooth and non-frizzy. Then I tried on about ten different pairs of jeans and leggings before deciding that a pair of my slightly faded older ones looked best with my Tigers T-shirt.

I kept going back and forth between two lotion scents: vanilla almond or orange blossom. Finally I chose vanilla almond, and I decided to take a major risk and wear some coppery earrings I'd never worn before.

However, I didn't take the risk of not wearing my glasses (even though I thought I looked much better without them). I wanted to actually be able to *see* Joey's tiger, right?

Before leaving, I stopped by the long silver mirror in our hallway just to give myself one last pep talk. I smiled at the person in the glass. *You can do this. It will be fun.*

Maybe it was the hazy light in the hallway or the effect of the earrings, but I thought I looked less serious and more sparkly than usual.

I tilted my head and smiled.

Yes, there was definitely something different about me. Usually I couldn't look in a mirror for more than a few seconds without noticing all the flaws and feeling embarrassed and having to look away.

Now the person in the mirror gazed right back with this kind of bold and confident look—as if to say: *I'm smart and funny, and I'm a good person, and I dare you not to like me.*

Sucking in my breath, I pulled my shoulders back more. Could I look even taller?

My brother suddenly appeared behind me in the hallway. I spun around.

"Whoa! You smell like a freaking vanilla farm," he said, grinning. "Hot date tonight?"

"No," I retorted, feeling my face getting warm. "Just stop it."

"Okay, okay. Don't be such a loser." He put on his mirrored sunglasses and picked up the keys from the table beside the front door. "Let's go."

Luke wasn't great at backing up, so it took two tries to get out of the driveway. Once we were headed down the road, he opened the windows and turned up the volume of the song he was playing on his iPod. I hunched down in my seat to keep my hair from blowing around too much—and because I couldn't stand his music.

After a few streets, Luke looked over at me and said, "Seriously, do you have a date tonight?"

"No," I replied with a glare. "I just wanted to look nice for the game because I'm helping out with the pregame stuff. Is that okay?"

I don't think my brother had any clue about Joey—or how I was one of the people who'd discovered him.

"Hey, I don't care," Luke said, half shrugging. "None of my business, but I'm just saying—most guys are jerks. Don't let yourself get hurt by some guy, that's all I'm saying." He grinned. "And hey, if you ever need me to beat someone up for you, I will."

Okay, I have to admit this whole conversation—even though it was kind of uncomfortable to have with my seventeen-year-old brother in a car—was also kind of sweet. It reminded me of the way he used to be.

"Thanks," I said. "But I'm not dating *anyone*, so it doesn't matter."

"Just saying," Luke finished. "I'm always here for you, Sis."

After circling the high school parking lot three or four times, looking for some of his friends' cars, he finally dropped me off at the gate. People were just starting to trickle into the stadium.

"Have fun. Stay out of trouble," he said, as I opened the door to get out.

I rolled my eyes. "Thanks, Dad."

Then he zoomed away to hang out with his friends—who weren't into football or Homecoming or Joey Byrd at all.

Of course, the first person I ran into was Julie Vanderbrook. She was walking into the stadium ahead of me with a couple of other sixth-grade girls. *Great.*

"Hey, April. I heard you're sitting with us tonight," she said in this friendly way when we caught up with each other beyond the gate. I couldn't tell if she'd heard about Noah, but knowing Julie, I would guess she probably did.

"Yeah, I think so," I said vaguely. I waved an arm toward the field. "But I'm helping with the pregame show and Joey first."

"Oh, I love Joey. He's so sweet—and his art is amazing," Julie said in this sincere-sounding voice. "You're lucky you get to help out with him. And hey—I like your earrings," she added, pointing at them.

Weirdly, this comment also sounded pretty sincere. Was it an act? Or was Julie trying to be nicer to me? I noticed her pink-streaked hair was gone, even though she still wore too much eye makeup for being a sixth grader.

"Thanks," I said awkwardly.

"Hey, good luck with Joey. I'll see you later in the stands." Waving, she disappeared into the crowd with her new group of girlfriends.

Honestly, I wanted to stay mad at her. I wanted to hate her new friends, and her new look, and her stylish clothes, and how she had treated me at the beginning of the school year—but I couldn't.

Why not? I guess because it felt like we were all changing. It wasn't just Julie and her friends. It was me too. Our outlines kept moving and changing every day—and there was no telling who we would eventually become.

April: One Tiny Orange-Armed Speck

Veena and Mr. Ulysses were already waiting on the sidelines when I got there.

"Hi, kiddo." Mr. Ulysses looked up when I reached them. Leaning on one knee, he was tinkering with a wheel on the chalk machine. "Don't you look spiffy for the game tonight!"

Then Veena came over and pointed at my copper earrings. "They are very beautiful. Are they new?" She leaned closer to inspect them.

"Yes," I said, feeling embarrassed by all the attention. "Where's Joey?" I asked, glancing around.

"Over there." Mr. Ulysses pointed.

Farther away, Joey was walking slowly along the sideline by himself. He didn't look nervous. Just focused—as if the white line was a narrow plank with quicksand on either side. What was he thinking about? I wondered. He wore the same clothes from school that day—the Tigers coat over a faded *Star Wars* T-shirt, with a pair of navy-blue sweatpants and white sneakers.

As he walked along the sideline, a few of the high school football players came out of the locker rooms and started to do some stretches on the field. One or two waved at Joey.

At the same time, the marching band was warming up in the Tigers end zone in their orange-and-black uniforms. The evening sun glinted off the trumpets and trombones. I could see some of the Homecoming floats lining up on the stadium's running track. My skin prickled with excitement.

We were here.

I was here.

"Okay, gang," Mr. Mac called out when he finally arrived with a big camera slung around his neck and a pizza box in his hands. "Sorry I'm late. Had to stop and pick up a little dinner for myself. Let's all have a quick meeting over here before things get too crazy." He motioned us toward the Tigers bench.

After he collected Joey from the sideline, Mr. Ulysses came over to join us. I saw him give Joey a smile and a quick thumbs-up as they walked together. I could tell the janitor was as excited as the rest of us.

"Okay, here's the game plan, gang." Mr. Mac pulled a wrinkled sheet of notebook paper out of his jeans pocket and unfolded it. "First, the football team will do their pre-game warm-ups." He glanced toward the field, which was now full of football players from both teams doing drills. Footballs sailed back and forth through the air.

"After that," he continued, "the announcer will welcome the crowd and introduce the Homecoming Court and the floats. Then we'll have the national anthem. Then the band"—he pointed in the direction of the band—"will do their pregame show. Three numbers. When that's finished, they'll move to the end zone to give Joey the whole field. After that, Joey will finish the show with an awesome Marshallville Tiger." He grinned at Joey. "The most impressive tiger the world has ever seen. Right, kiddo?"

Joey nodded.

"You forgot to mention something else that will happen," Mr. Ulysses added with a sly grin.

"What's that?" Mr. Mac asked.

"Joey will help Marshallville win by a score of 50–0."

Everybody laughed because they knew that would definitely never happen.

Joey smiled at Mr. Ulysses's joke, although he didn't really seem to be paying attention to the conversation. His eyes wandered toward the field, and up to the lights, and in the direction of the band, which was rehearsing one of their songs. Batons flew in the distance, spinning like bright pinwheels against the sky.

"What would you like for us to do now?" Veena asked in her organized way.

Mr. Mac put his hands on his hips as he surveyed everything. "Good question. I guess what I was envisioning was that we would stay on the sidelines to give Joey some moral support, and I'd take some pictures of the tiger while he's working on it. But that's not exactly going to work from ground level, is it?" The counselor squinted at the field.

"What about from the top of the stands?" Veena pointed at the grandstand that rose steeply behind us. We had a larger grandstand than a lot of schools because it was used for other events throughout the year. The rows were already filling up with people. "If you and Mr. Ulysses want to stay with Joey, April and I could take pictures from up there for you." She gestured toward the top rows.

Right away, I started to panic. I didn't want to go to the top of the stands. How could I leave Veena there by herself after the show?

"Great idea." Mr. Mac nodded. "It's the school's camera, so you can return it on Monday if I don't see you guys later on."

"Actually, I'm not sure how long I'll be able to stay," I kind of mumbled, but I don't think anybody heard me. Mr. Mac started showing Veena how to work the camera. Mr. Ulysses stooped over to adjust a wheel on the art machine.

I shook my head. How was any of this going to work out?

Nearby, Joey fidgeted with the extra-long sleeves of his coat—pushing them up and down.

I moved over to him. "You okay?" I asked.

"Yeah, I'm good," he said with one of his nervous shrugs.

Trying to ignore my own problems, I gave him a last-minute pep talk. "Just remember to ignore the crowd even if they're really loud," I said. "All you have to do is pretend you're on Marshallville's playground at recess and stay focused and concentrate like you normally do. Just do your best and I know everybody will love you."

"Okay." Joey nodded.

Veena spoke up from behind me. "And we'll make sure to take lots of pictures of your design." After she put Mr. Mac's camera around her neck, she pointed at the grandstands. "Remember to look for us. We'll wave at you, okay?"

"Okay." Joey nodded again.

Then Mr. Ulysses motioned for Joey to follow him. "Well, we better give this art machine of yours a practice run-through along the sidelines before everything gets too busy."

Impulsively, I reached out to shake Joey's hand before he left. "For good luck," I said.

Awkwardly, Joey shook my hand and Veena's hand— and even Mr. Mac's.

As we started up the steps into the grandstand, I glanced back over my shoulder to check on Joey one last time. I don't know why, but I had this weird feeling that this was the last time I would see him.

He was walking next to Mr. Ulysses, who was pushing the chalk machine down the sideline. Mr. Mac followed a few steps behind them, talking on his cell phone. Football players and coaches swarmed everywhere. Reaching up to catch a practice throw, one player came flying toward Joey.

My breath caught in my chest. I could see disaster unfolding in slow motion with Joey, the football player, and the art machine.

Fortunately, the player somehow sidestepped Joey at

the last minute. The ball sailed harmlessly over Joey's head and ricocheted off the Tigers bench.

Crisis averted.

But the scene reminded me again how crazy this whole idea was. How could we expect one small fourth grader to entertain an entire stadium with his art? What kind of impossible magic were we asking Joey to do? He was just a tiny orange-armed speck moving bravely through a churning ocean of padded shoulders and helmets and flying footballs and chaos.

A lump rose in my throat. I had no idea what would happen during the show or what the outcome would be—I only hoped he would survive.

JOEYBYRD

From above, Marshallville's football stadium looked beautiful. It winked like an emerald under the artificial lights. At night you could see it from miles away, even when the rest of the landscape had faded into darkness.

The stadium was the center of life in Marshallville, Michigan. Drama and heartbreak, victory and defeat, love and loss—all wrapped up in one neat box. And sometimes, if everything went right, it was the place where legends were made.

For Joey Byrd, this will be true.

April: Above

I could barely keep up as Veena climbed higher and higher. Clearly, I wasn't as fit (or speedy) as she was. Instead, I kept bumping into people and having to say "excuse me" and "sorry" about every five seconds. My legs burned from the climb.

Of course, Veena went to the very last row at the top of the grandstands. Behind us, there was nothing except a corrugated metal wall with the words TIGER COUNTRY written on it.

And air.

I wasn't a big fan of steep heights like this at all. When we finally reached the top, I had to literally force myself to turn around. Even then, I held on to one of the metal handrails with one hand for security.

"Are you okay?" Veena asked, noticing my anxious expression.

"Sure." But I couldn't really relax and look around until I was sitting down on the bleachers.

As we waited for the pregame events to start, Veena practiced taking a few pictures with the camera. "Everything is so colorful," she said excitedly.

"Like India?" I teased.

"Yes," she nodded, eyes sparkling. "It is."

Which just goes to show you that home can be found anywhere.

Below us, the stadium was a moving kaleidoscope of colors and shapes. You didn't know where to look first. Homecoming convertibles in shades of candy-apple red and turquoise-blue waited to parade past the stands. Football players filled the field with shifting patterns of orange and black, and blue and silver, as they went through their warm-ups. Cheerleaders backflipped along the sidelines and tossed silver pom-poms into the air.

Although I'd been to other Homecomings before, this one seemed different. Maybe it was the view from the top of the grandstand, but the whole scene seemed much more colorful and exciting than I remembered.

I couldn't help wondering if this was the way Joey saw the world all the time. Was it always this chaotic, confusing, colorful scene to him? And were there other ways of seeing it—ones that we hadn't even discovered yet?

I must have spoken the last question out loud, because Veena turned to me and suddenly said, "Yes."

"What?" I glanced at her.

"You asked if there were other ways of seeing, and I was answering—yes, there are." She lowered Mr. Mac's camera. "In India, we believe in something called the third eye." She tapped a spot between her eyes. "It is here. It is the mind's eye—the invisible eye of intuition and intellect that looks inward."

Wow. I loved that idea. A third eye that looked inward.

"That's exactly how I see the world sometimes."

Veena smiled. "Everyone has one."

It made me think about other ways of seeing things that weren't visible—like thoughts and feelings. Could we see with our heart for instance? Was there a heart's eye?

Suddenly, the stadium loudspeaker crackled. My heart skipped a few beats as I realized the field had mostly cleared.

It was time.

"Gooood evening, Marshallville! Welcome to tonight's Homecoming game! Let's hear it for our Marshallville Tigers team," the announcer called out, and the crowd roared in response.

As the sound rolled upward, I started to panic. I couldn't see Joey or the art machine anywhere on the sideline. Where was he? Had it been too much for him already?

Below us, the activities moved at a dizzying pace. Convertibles and floats rolled past the stands. There was the introduction of the Homecoming Court. The presentation of the King and Queen—a football player and a cheerleader (of course). The national anthem. The band routines.

Veena took pictures of everything—although I was sure Mr. Mac didn't really need photos of the Homecoming Court or the parade of convertibles from Marshallville Ford. But Veena was so excited, I didn't want to ruin her happiness.

And then—before I realized what was happening—the announcer was introducing Joey.

"And now, folks, we have a big surprise for you to-night," the voice boomed over the stadium. "I want you to turn your attention to the field and see what Marshallville Elementary's most famous artist has in store for us tonight. You've seen him on TV. You've read about him in the newspaper. Everybody, put your hands together for fourth grader Joey Byrd and his fantastic Art Machine."

My heart leaped into my throat.

I could see Joey on the sideline now. He stood motion-less on the fifty-yard line marker. His small body was nearly swallowed up by the orange-and-black Tigers coat. As the crowd roared for him, I could see the coat sway a little, as if the sound itself might topple him like a house of cards.

I clenched my hands together.

Please, please stay vertical, I whispered.

I saw Mr. Ulysses step out from the crowd on the side-line to squeeze Joey's shoulder. He appeared to whisper something in his ear. Whatever he said seemed to work. After a slight hesitation, Joey entered the field, slowly pushing the gleaming chalk machine in front of him.

From above, the orange tank was vivid against the emerald-green grass. The stadium lights glinted off the brass funnel. As Joey moved into the open field, a bright line of white chalk dust trailed behind him.

An expectant hush fell over the crowd.

I was sure most fans had already guessed what Joey Byrd was about to make (although I still had my own doubts).

There was no question it would be a Marshallville Tiger. How good would it be? How long would it take? Those were the only real mysteries.

What did appear on the field that legendary Homecoming night was a surprise to everyone. Even today, it is still a matter of much debate.

JOEYBYRD

Human beings can't fly like eagles. Chalk tigers can't roar. Except in dreams and movies. Still, Joey thought it might be possible. If the wings were big enough. If his tracing was perfect enough. If someone's imagination was strong enough. Perhaps the magic could happen. Perhaps you could see a tiger, or an eagle— or something else entirely.

It would all depend on where you looked from.

April: What We Saw

From our vantage point at the top of the stands, we had a bird's-eye view of everything Joey did. Aiming Mr. Mac's camera at the field, Veena stood on tiptoe—as if that would somehow help her take better pictures.

At first, Joey seemed to be heading in the right direction—moving clockwise around the field making the wavy outline of the tiger's furry head. Mr. Ulysses's chalk machine seemed to be working perfectly. The lines un-spooled behind Joey like bright strands of thread. And he seemed to be walking faster than usual—which was good, because I wasn't sure how patient the crowd would be.

I let myself relax a little. Everything was going perfectly so far.

The stands on both sides of the field were so quiet that you could hear the sound of seagulls screeching in the parking lot.

As Joey reached the opposite side of the field, the play-ers on both football teams climbed up on their benches to get a better view. It seemed funny to see the big high school football players—some the size of small mountains—focused on a little kid in an orange-sleeved coat.

As Joey turned toward us again, I expected the details of the tiger's face to begin emerging at any moment. I waited for the fierce eyes and the diagonal whiskers and the stripes to appear. . . .

But they didn't.

That's when I started to get worried.

What was Joey doing?

I whispered to Veena, "What in the world is he making?"

"I'm not sure," she replied, keeping her eyes on the screen of the camera.

A murmur grew among the crowd as people began to stand up, row by row, trying to get a better view—trying to decipher what they were seeing.

Pretty soon everyone in the bleachers (including me) was standing. Next to us, the announcers in the broadcast booth leaned out their open window.

Was the fourth grader making a wing or a paw? Was it a nose or a beak? Human or animal? Vegetable or mineral? No one was quite certain. Hands pointed. Voices grew louder. Phones balanced in midair, trying to capture a good picture.

I could see Mr. Ulysses and Mr. Mac standing on the sidelines, arms folded, as if they weren't sure what to do. At the top of the grandstand, we were just as helpless.

Joey kept walking.

His gaze never seemed to waver from the field. He never looked around. A plastic grocery bag tumbled across the grass in front of him. He didn't pause.

As more time passed, the crowd grew more restless. Patience began to evaporate. My stomach knotted inside me. I could tell things were on the verge of falling apart.

Then Joey moved to the center of the field and stopped. As everyone grew quiet again, he pushed the art machine off to one side of the fifty-yard line. Was he finished? Taking a break? Giving up? No one knew.

The crowd on our side of the field began to chant, "Joey! Joey!" as if to encourage him to keep going. On the Kenston side, they picked it up too.

Acknowledging nothing, Joey zipped up his Tigers coat and lay down flat on the fifty-yard line. Surrounded by the tangle of mysterious chalk lines he'd made, he spread out his arms and stared faceup at the sky.

And at that moment, something strange happened in the stadium.

I swear a crackle of energy spun through the air. My neck prickled and my arms broke out in goose bumps. I felt dizzy and warm for a second or two.

At the same time, the tangle of chalk-white lines covering the field suddenly made sense. I don't know how else to describe it, except to say that the lines *became* a tiger. Somehow. One minute they pictured nothing—and the next minute, a tiger the size of a football field seemed to stare (or blink?) up at the sky.

Not everyone saw it—some people did, and some didn't. A few people insisted the tiger was so real that they even heard it roar.

I was one of them.

"Wow! Look at that tiger!" I shouted to Veena.

"Yes," she replied, after a strange hesitation.

On the opposite side of the field, the Kenston fans saw something entirely different. Later on, we'd hear stories of how a magnificent eagle appeared in front of them and stretched out its wings from end zone to end zone. Some fans said they felt a brief sensation of floating. Others insisted they saw and felt nothing at all.

Of course, while all this was happening on the field—while everybody was trying to understand what they were seeing and not seeing—Joey Byrd and his art disappeared.

April: Erased

At first, I didn't realize Joey was gone.

Like everyone else, I was fumbling with my phone. I was trying to hold the screen high enough to capture everything on the field, which wasn't easy considering all of the people who were doing the same thing.

But the chance to take a picture was gone in an instant.

Almost as soon as Joey finished his design, a dazzling burst of fireworks exploded above the scoreboard to mark the start of the game. As the grandstand erupted in cheers, both teams leaped off their benches and galloped onto the field.

In seconds, Joey's creation vanished in a cloud of chalk dust beneath their feet.

Only his Tigers coat remained untouched on the fifty-yard line—although it took me a few minutes to realize he wasn't inside it any longer. Like I said—there were fireworks going off, and people cheering, and football players high-fiving one another.

Once I realized Joey's coat was there, but he wasn't, I turned to Veena in panic. "Where's Joey?" I shouted over the crowd noise.

"What?" she said.

I waved one arm at the field. "Look! His coat is still there, but he isn't. Where did he go?"

"I don't know." Veena stood on her tiptoes to survey the field. "I don't see him either. Perhaps he just forgot his coat on the field by accident." She pointed out Mr. Ulysses, who was pushing the art machine off the field. "Look. Mr. Ulysses is already down there. He'll pick it up, I'm sure. Maybe Joey left with Mr. Mac or his parents already."

Minutes later, a referee retrieved the coat and brought it to the sideline where he handed it to a coach. Although I knew Veena was probably right about Joey leaving with his parents or Mr. Mac, I kept scanning the field for him until the game started—until it was clear he must have left.

As our team completed its first couple of plays on the field, I have to admit I wasn't paying much attention to what was going on. I was still thinking about Joey and the tiger and the coat and everything that happened.

Had a tiger really appeared on the field? Had it moved? Had it roared?

"Joey's drawing was pretty amazing, wasn't it?" I shouted to Veena between plays.

"What?" she said, leaning closer again to hear me over all the noise.

"Joey's tiger was amazing, wasn't it?" I repeated.

"Yes," she nodded, her eyes wide and unblinking behind her aqua glasses. "I did not expect it to be like that."

Veena didn't tell me what she had *actually* seen until a couple of days later. That's when she admitted that she never saw the tiger. For Veena, the lines had been a breathtaking eagle—

213

and for a few seconds, she'd felt as if she were flying. "The stadium looked like a glittering jewel box below me," she told me. "I was so startled I almost dropped Mr. Mac's camera."

Honestly, nobody had much time to talk about what they'd seen. Once the game got under way, it was so exciting, you had to pay attention. Our team scored its first touchdown on the opening drive and the stands went crazy with cheering and celebration. More fireworks burst above the scoreboard, and that's when I knew I needed to find the sixth graders soon—before I missed everything and Noah had totally given up on me.

But what should I do about Veena? That was the dilemma.

I couldn't just leave her at the top of the grandstand by herself. She was a fifth grader and she was from India and she'd never been to a football game in her life. But it also seemed rude to send her to sit with her parents. I wasn't like Julie Vanderbrook. I couldn't abandon people.

I sighed. I would have to bring her with me. There was no other option. "Hey, I think I'm going to go and sit with some people from sixth grade," I said to Veena. "I don't know how many extra seats they'll have saved, but you can come if you want to."

I'll be honest—I really hoped Veena would say no.

She didn't.

Instead, her whole face lit up. "Really? I would be honored to do that," she said, pushing her dark hair behind her ears and smiling. "I don't know any other sixth graders except you."

I held back another sigh. "We aren't very exciting," I said. "You'll see."

April: Section E

The grandstand was a complete mob scene. I had no idea how Veena and I would ever stick together and find Section E. On the field, Marshallville kept making fantastic plays, so all the high schoolers kept standing up and cheering. Trying to find anyone—or hear anything—was almost impossible.

Jacob had said Section E was in the upper bleachers behind the high school band. Of course, the band was at the opposite end of the big grandstand from us. It took forever to get there. We had to go down the bleacher steps and across the front of the grandstand.

Once we reached the right side, I stopped to scan the upper bleachers. It was an endless wall of orange-and-black shirts. I couldn't see a single face I recognized. It was hopeless.

"I don't think they're even up there," I shouted at Veena over the noise of the crowd. "I don't see anyone I recognize."

"Well, we can just try going to the top and see if we find anyone," she said.

Honestly, if it had been up to me, I probably would have turned around and given up. So maybe there was an advantage to having Veena there for encouragement and moral support.

I started climbing the concrete steps, but it was almost impossible to look for the sixth graders and concentrate on not tripping over any high schoolers' feet at the same time.

We had nearly reached the top when someone on my left shouted, "Hey, April and Veena!"

I glanced in the direction of the voice.

Rochelle was sitting on the end of a row waving wildly at us as if we were long-lost friends. "Hey, you want to sit with us?" she shouted.

I was about to reply *No, but thanks anyway* when I realized that she was surrounded by sixth graders. Rachel and a row of girls sat next to her. A bunch of sixth-grade boys, including Tanner and Jacob, were crammed, knee to knee, in the row behind them. I couldn't see Noah at first, but I didn't really have time to look because our team made another touchdown and the stands erupted with cheers.

Except for one small space at the end of the bleacher, you couldn't squeeze another body into the row.

"Okay, thanks. We'll take it," I said to Rochelle, thinking how ironic it was that the girl who stole my markers in kindergarten was offering me a seat now. Was it a fair trade? A seat (six years later) for my stolen markers? I wasn't sure.

Veena and I sandwiched ourselves onto the end of the group. When the Tigers scored again and everybody leaped up to cheer, I turned around to see if I could locate

Noah Langley somewhere in the boys' row behind us, but I couldn't find him.

After that, I kind of gave up looking.

I told myself that maybe he had chickened-out and skipped the game. Or maybe he couldn't find a seat. Or possibly it had all been a joke.

If that was true—well, I would show Noah and Jacob: I'd have a great time anyway.

Which I did.

I screamed and cheered until I was hoarse. And I did the wave. And I took a bunch of selfies with Veena and the two Rs and the other girls in our row. Rachel offered to write *Go Tigers!* on my face in black eyeliner, so I let her. All the sixth-grade girls had orange tiger paws and *Go Tigers!* written on their faces. Veena got a *Go Tigers!* too.

By halftime, the score was 28–0 in favor of the Tigers. Which was crazy. Kenston had a bigger (and better) team than us, and we were totally crushing them. I started to wonder if Joey's tiger was working its magic and we'd actually win 50–0 like Mr. Ulysses had predicted.

At halftime, a lot of the girls decided to walk around the stadium and see the floats up close. Veena went with Rochelle and Rachel, but I decided to stay and save our seats.

Right after they left, I felt a soft bump on my arm. I turned around thinking maybe it was Julie, since I hadn't spotted her in the stands yet—

Noah Langley stood right behind me. *Oh my gosh.*

"Hey," he said in a rush, his face scarlet-red. "Hey, I

was wondering if you wanted to go and get some nachos with me or something?"

My insides felt like a whole stadium of dazzling fireworks.

"Sure," I said, doing my best to sound calm and normal. "That would be fun."

I didn't mention a word about saving seats. It didn't matter anyway. There were plenty of sixth graders around.

Of course, it took forever to get to the concession area with all the crowds. Noah stayed in front of me, and I just concentrated on not slamming into him by accident—or losing sight of his orange shirt among a million other ones.

When the crowd finally thinned out, he stopped and leaned on a railing, waiting for me to catch up. "Wow, I can't believe you didn't get, like, lost," he said.

"Human GPS," I answered, and then winced inside because maybe that was a dumb thing to say.

Surprisingly, Noah laughed at my lame joke and then pointed toward the long concession lines snaking in front of the stadium gates. "Popcorn or nachos?"

Since I wasn't a huge fan of chemical-orange cheese, I said popcorn.

"Okay," he agreed.

As we stood together in the popcorn line, it was kind of awkward coming up with things to say at first. We started talking about the crowd and which sixth graders we'd seen so far—and then we got to the pregame show.

"What did you think of Joey's tiger?" I asked.

Noah described how unbelievable it looked from where he sat. "It reminded me of one of those Etch A Sketch things. At first the lines didn't look like anything."

"I know," I agreed.

"But Joey kept pushing that bizarre machine around, and little by little, you could see things you recognized. Then he lay down on the field and the tiger kind of appeared around him somehow. And then all the fireworks went off. It was so, so cool. I don't know how he did it, but it was really amazing."

Noah pulled out his phone. "Here—I'll show you some pictures I took of it." He flipped through a few blurry pictures that mostly showed the backs of people's heads in the stands and some vague white lines on the field. "I guess nothing came out very good," he said, squinting at his phone. "I think it must have been the lighting. Or I'm a really, really bad photographer." Noah grinned and shook his head.

For the first time, I noticed that he had braces. (Which just goes to show you that I don't notice everything.)

"Did you get any good pictures?" he asked.

I showed him the pathetic ones on my phone, which were just as blurry.

In fact, it wasn't just our pictures that were bad.

Turns out, *no one* captured the precise moment when Joey finished his design—not even the local newspaper photographer, or Veena, who took about a million pictures for Mr. Mac with our school's camera.

Every single photo of Joey's artwork that night was too

dark or too blurry. Or it was obscured by hands or heads. Or it didn't look like anything recognizable—just white scribbles on the grass.

Opinions would vary about why this was the case. Was it the slope of the grandstand? Or the artificial lights? Or the flash from the fireworks? Or the chalk being too light? Or the field being too dark?

Later on, I would come to the conclusion that maybe Joey's Homecoming creation wasn't supposed to be saved on film. Maybe it was supposed to be a rare moment, a fleeting gift. Like a sunset. Or a rainbow. Or a shooting star. You had to see it for yourself with your own eyes—and even then, you would always wish you had a picture to prove what you saw. But there was no proof.

You just had to be there.

April: Sparkling Popcorn

Noah Langley and I spent nearly all of halftime waiting in the popcorn line.

I didn't really mind.

As the line crept toward the front, we talked about a lot more stuff: sixth grade, sports, a language arts assignment we had for the weekend, and what flavor to get on the popcorn. (Barbecue.) Noah checked his phone and texted a few times, which made me a little nervous. Was he texting about us?

Being me, I had to ask him. "What are you texting about?"

Noah blushed a little and shoved his phone into his pocket. "Actually, I'm texting my dad back because he wants to know where I'm sitting." He rolled his eyes. "I told my parents to leave me alone, but they never listen."

I laughed. "Mine are like that too."

By the time we finally got our popcorn, the third quarter was already underway. Instead of fighting our way back to the seats, Noah suggested watching the game along the end zone fence while we shared the popcorn.

I said, "Sure."

Although the view was great from that end of the field, we ended up talking to each other more than watching the game. I have no idea how many times our team scored, or who scored, or anything.

What I did notice was how everything seemed super-bright and kind of sparkly—me, Noah, the stadium, the neon-green field stretching away to infinity—even the red stripes on the popcorn bucket.

We talked about everything. I found out Noah collected vinyl records and old license plates. "I've got every U.S. license plate, and ones from France, England, and Germany," he told me. "And I'm getting a really cool one from Italy for my birthday this year."

I told him how I liked researching and reading about virtually anything.

"And writing advice columns, right?" he joked. Then his face reddened as he said, "Sorry for my lame letter. I hope you didn't think it was weird."

"No, it was cute," I said. "But I didn't know it was from you until Jacob said it."

Noah rolled his eyes and grinned. "He's such an idiot."

Then there was this long silence until Noah noticed that it was almost the end of the third quarter.

"We should probably go back to our seats to watch the end of the game," he said.

"Yeah, we're almost out of popcorn," I agreed, shaking the bucket, which was almost empty. I couldn't believe how much we'd eaten.

Then Noah mumbled really fast, "Maybe, if you want,

we could sit together or something at the next home game. I think there are two games left."

All of a sudden I panicked. Did I want to sit with Noah Langley? Did that mean he liked me? Did I want everyone to know he liked me? Did I like him?

An answer blurted out of my mouth before I could stop it. "Actually, it was fun just standing around here talking and eating popcorn. Maybe we could do something like that again at the next game?"

I don't know if it was my imagination or not, but I thought Noah looked relieved.

"Yeah, okay, that sounds good." He smiled. "I'll take some pictures of my collection to show you next time."

"I think my dad has an old license plate from Ontario in the garage," I added. "He used to have a fishing cabin there. I'll see if I can bring it to school for you."

"That would be great. Maybe I'll start a Canadian collection next." Noah grinned. The stadium lights glinted off his braces. They had tiny green wires, I noticed. For some reason, this made me like him even more.

"Thanks—this was really fun," I said, hoping that's what I was supposed to say.

"Sure," he said.

Then we went back to our seats.

Although Noah kind of ignored me after that, he did look in my direction once before he left at the end of the game with Tanner and his friends. (At least I think he looked in my direction.)

Honestly, it was one of the best nights of my life—

well, up to that point in my life anyway. Everything that happened seemed so magical and almost unreal when I thought about it later. Joey's tiger. Watching the game with the sixth graders. Eating popcorn with Noah.

And the game went down in the history books of Marshallville, Michigan, as the largest Homecoming win. Ever.

Unbelievably, the final score was 50–0, just as Mr. Ulysses had predicted.

JOEYBYRD

Not all birds migrate, but many do. Scientists believe some birds carry an invisible compass inside them—bits of magnetic dust and instinct that tell them when it's time to go. Some migrate in daylight. Others travel under the cover of darkness.

Like birds, Joey's parents moved around a lot.

Sometimes they moved to protect Joey from problems at school or with other kids. Sometimes they moved to get a change of scenery or a fresh start. Sometimes they moved just because they were the kind of people who liked to be left alone.

After the game on Friday, Joey and his family started packing. They didn't have much. They always traveled light.

On Saturday afternoon, they left Marshallville and started driving south.

April: Instant Fame

Monday morning. Everybody wanted to congratulate Joey for the game.

Before the school day started, the star quarterback of the Tigers football team drove over from the high school to drop off Joey's forgotten coat, along with an autographed game ball from the team.

As kids drifted in from the buses and the car line, Joey's locker stopped traffic. It was completely covered with colorful streamers and balloons and signs. Apparently, the decorations were the work of the high school cheerleaders.

During morning announcements, Ms. Getzhammer gave a short speech about how proud Marshallville Elementary was of Joey Byrd. "His lucky tiger won the game for us," she said. Even though that was probably a *slight* exaggeration, cheers echoed down the halls.

Despite all the praise that was waiting to be showered on him, Joey never showed up for school that day.

When he didn't appear at recess—when nobody in a familiar red jacket slipped through the glass doors—I had the feeling that I'd been right after all. I'd sensed Joey wasn't coming back when he walked away from us before the pregame show. Maybe it was my intuition—my mind's eye, as Veena would say. The empty coat Joey had left on the fifty-yard line only added to that belief.

Of course, the bracelet girls pestered me with questions. Was Joey sick? Was he on vacation? Was he too famous to come to school now?

They decided to draw a giant picture on the playground to show Joey how much they missed him. It was kind of ironic, considering how badly they had once treated him.

The girls spent about ten minutes arguing about what to make:

"How about a tiger?"

"No, that's too hard and ours would look dumb compared to his."

"How about a crying emoji?"

"Why?"

"Because everybody misses him."

"What if he doesn't get what it means?"

"How about a crying emoji and the words 'We miss you, Joey'?"

"Okay."

After dividing up the different parts of the design, the fourth-grade girls made a lopsided face with a big teardrop between the Buddy Bench and the swing sets.

I think they expected that Joey would magically appear when they finished it.

He didn't.

In fact, nothing changed that day. Or the next one.

I think everyone (except me) believed that Joey would show up eventually. After all, his name was plastered all over Marshallville. Tickets for the two remaining home games sold out in less than twenty-four hours. Everyone wanted to see what Joey would do at the next game and how outrageous the score would be.

But I kept wondering what would happen if Joey did come back. Would people expect something even better? Would the tiger be as surprising, as special, the second time around? What if our team lost? Would Joey be blamed?

On Wednesday morning, Veena stopped me in the hallway.

She told me that she'd asked Mr. Ulysses and Mr. Mac if they knew where Joey was. Mr. Mac said he'd tried calling Joey's house on Tuesday and nobody answered. He told Veena that maybe they'd had a family emergency or they went on a trip or something. Mr. Ulysses told Veena not to worry—that he was sure everything would work out fine.

"He didn't seem very concerned," Veena said. Which we thought was odd.

On Thursday, I reached into my Advice Box and I was surprised to find another drawing from Joey Byrd.

Or so I thought.

April: The Drawing

The drawing was on a piece of notebook paper folded into a precise square. I almost missed it. The box was packed with a bunch of other notes that I emptied out first—mostly crayon messages written by little kids asking where Joey was or how to find him.

Then the square of paper fell at my feet.

Picking it up from the hallway, I opened up the note and smoothed it out on my math textbook to read what it said. When I saw the spirals and squares, I immediately thought it had to be from Joey, even though it was more detailed than his old drawings. And it had writing on it.

There was a large circle marked TREE in the center of the page. The upper corner of the page had a small spiral. In another corner, there was a sketch of something square with the words JOEY'S TOWER written next to it. Another part was labeled NEW SWINGS. A small rectangle said GARDEN, with a little row of sprouts.

It took me a few seconds to realize it was a map of our school playground.

Only, Joey hadn't drawn it the way it was now—he'd imagined *how he wanted it to be*. He'd turned Marshallville's tired, old rundown playground into a completely different place with new climbing equipment, new swings, a garden . . .

I was so excited by the discovery that I tracked down Mr. Ulysses to show him the drawing during morning announcements. He was mopping the entrance hallway because it was a slushy day and there were puddles everywhere.

"Look," I said, waving the paper to get his attention. "Joey left another note for me."

Mr. Ulysses seemed confused. "What?"

"I found a new drawing from Joey in my Advice Box today," I explained as I handed the paper to him. "I think it's his idea for a new playground for us."

Mr. Ulysses pulled a pair of bifocals from his shirt pocket and put them on. "Hmmm . . . ," he said as he studied the drawing. He turned the paper over to see the back of it. "So—except for the words JOEY'S TOWER on the front, his name isn't written anywhere else on this page, right?"

"No," I said. I didn't think it mattered.

"Hmmm . . ." The janitor gazed upward as if he was thinking. I had the feeling he was trying to decide whether to tell me something or not. Finally, he said, "I've got to be honest with you, April—I don't think this could be from Joey."

"Why not?"

Mr. Ulysses hesitated a long time before answering slowly. "Well, because I happen to know that Joey and his family moved away last weekend. That's why." He pushed his mop through an invisible puddle of water on the floor.

I exhaled slowly. So I'd been right.

"I didn't want to be the one to say anything because I felt it was up to Joey's parents to let the school know," Mr. Ulysses continued, looking guilty. "I thought they would call Ms. Getzhammer when they got to wherever they were headed and let everybody know. But I guess they haven't given the school any word yet."

I tried not to sound hurt that the janitor hadn't told us (Veena or me) what he knew. "So how did you find out?"

"Joey told me right before the pregame show on Friday," Mr. Ulysses explained. "I asked him if he had any big plans for the weekend, and out of the clear blue sky he told me he was moving to Florida."

Florida.

I suddenly remembered the waves Joey had done during Friday's recess—how he'd covered the entire playground with swooping, curling lines. Had Joey been trying to give all of us a big hint then?

Mr. Ulysses shook his head. "I was as shocked as you are by the news. I hardly knew what to say when Joey told me. I asked him if he was sad about leaving, and he said, 'No, I move a lot. But I'll miss your art machine and the two nice girls at recess who always talked to me.'"

I squinted skeptically at Mr. Ulysses and he held up one hand. "That's an exact quote. I swear."

Then there was a long silence.

All my emotions seemed to be crashing into one another. Shock. Sadness. Guilt. Regret.

"I feel like it's my fault he had to leave," I said finally.

"What?" Mr. Ulysses gave me an incredulous look. "Why would you say that?"

"Because I was one of the people who told everyone about him." I tried to keep my voice from shaking. "Maybe if I'd just shut up and never mentioned him or pointed him out to anyone, he could have kept doing his art on the playground and been perfectly happy here."

I knew this sounded a little self-pitying, but that's how I felt at that moment.

The janitor bumped his mop into my shoes. "Now, that's just nonsense, April. You need to shape up and stop talking like that. Come over here and sit down with me so we can have a little chat." He pointed at the old wooden benches along the side of the school lobby. Above them was a display case of school honors. (Not that I'm bragging—but my name was on a couple of the plaques.)

"Okay, let's sit down here." Mr. Ulysses pushed the big box of Lost and Found items out of the way to make room for us. "First of all," he said, turning to me, "I'm sure it was Joey's parents who made the choice to leave, not him. But despite that—what if you finding Joey was the best thing that could have happened to him?"

I gave him a skeptical look. "How?"

Mr. Ulysses shrugged. "Because most of the rare birds never get discovered."

I had no idea what he was getting at.

"What do you mean?" I asked.

"Well, let's just say I've worked here at Marshallville for a long time," Mr. Ulysses said. "And I've seen literally thousands and thousands of kids come and go through those doors over the years." The janitor waved one hand toward the glass doors of the lobby entrance. "But every once in a while, a rare bird shows up. They are kids just like Joey with something different, something unique, something unfamiliar about them—kids who land here for a short period of time to see if anybody notices them."

He sighed and looked upward. "Usually no one does. Anything that is different or unusual makes most people uncomfortable. They stay as far away as they can. And before long, the rare bird gives up and moves on, and nobody knows the possibilities that they just missed."

Mr. Ulysses patted my arm. "But you spotted Joey. You found one of the rare birds—literally, a Byrd." He chuckled at his own joke. "And you and Veena didn't just find him. You helped other people to see what was extraordinary about him. And"—he pointed one finger at me—"you helped Joey to discover some things he didn't even know about himself."

"Like what?" I said, still feeling guilty.

"Like how he could relate to the outside world and other people. And how he was capable of doing more than he realized. You helped him to find his own possibilities—his own magic." Mr. Ulysses waved his arms for emphasis. "Those are big things."

"Okay, but then he left."

After a thoughtful pause, Mr. Ulysses replied, "Actually, I'd venture to say that he left at the perfect time. He left after he'd helped us to see a lot of things—but before his luster had a chance to fade. You know what I mean?"

I didn't want to admit it, but I understood exactly what he meant. I'd worried what fame (and Marshallville) would do to Joey and his art—how it might have changed him, or overwhelmed him, or even turned people against him eventually.

For the first time, it occurred to me how much Joey was like his own tracings: How he couldn't stay long. How he was mysterious and unforgettable, but also fragile and temporary. Just like chalk dust and earth.

Mr. Ulysses smiled and gently wagged a finger at me. "See, April, you may think you are as different as Joey sometimes. But you are more like the rest of the world than you think you are."

"So I'm not a rare bird?" I joked.

"Nope." Mr. Ulysses shook his head. "Not really. But you're the kind of person who isn't afraid of the mysteries and questions in life. You seek out what is unfamiliar and different. And you don't quit until you find the answers. That's why you saw Joey. And it'll be up to all of us to make sure that what he showed us doesn't get forgotten. . . ."

Feeling embarrassed by all the praise, I held up the pencil sketch again. "So you really think someone else did this playground design?"

"That would be my guess," the janitor said, squinting at it again.

"Who?" I wondered if it could have been someone like Noah, but that seemed unlikely. Why would he care about redesigning our school's playground?

"Who knows?" Mr. Ulysses shrugged.

"I'll find out," I promised as I stood up.

"I know you will." Mr. Ulysses grinned.

But I have to confess, as I walked back to class, I kept thinking about what Mr. Ulysses had said about me. Was I a rare bird or not? I wondered.

April: Veena's Secret

The next day, I showed Veena the playground map. When she sat down on the Buddy Bench with her lunch, I passed the folded-up drawing to her. "Before you do anything else—open up this note and see what you think."

Veena's eyes darted toward me with a strange look. "Why?"

"Open it. I want to know your opinion."

"Okay," she said finally. It was a cold day, so she was wearing pink gloves. It seemed to take forever for her to get the paper unfolded. Then she pressed the drawing flat on her lap and gazed at it for a few seconds with the same odd expression on her face.

"Do you know what it shows?" I prompted.

"No, I am not quite sure," she mumbled.

I pointed out some of the features—the spiral, the tree, the benches. I couldn't keep the excitement out of my voice. "I think it's supposed to be a design for a new playground for our school. Someone left it in my Advice Box yesterday. At first, I thought it had to be Joey. But it couldn't have been him because he hasn't been in school all week. So who do you think did it?"

Veena's pink-gloved hands fidgeted with the map. "Did you hear me?"

"Yes," she answered softly, without looking up.

"So who do you think did it?"

Veena stayed silent and kept staring uncomfortably at her gloves—and that's the moment I realized it had to be her.

I pointed at her. "Wait. You did it! You were the one who left it, weren't you?"

Veena covered her face with her hands. In a muffled voice, she said into the pinkness of her gloves, "Yes."

I tugged the paper off her lap. "So is this your idea for a new playground for Marshallville? Did you make this?"

Looking up from her gloves, Veena nodded. "Yes. I am very sorry," she said apologetically. "I kept thinking about how nice it would be to make the playground better for Joey when he came back. So I did a drawing of what I was thinking. It was like my dream of a playground," she added with an embarrassed smile.

She started pointing out some of the details on her map. The spiral of sadness path for kids to walk on. The three Buddy Benches instead of one—

"For more conversation," she explained.

She showed me how she wanted to replace our old jungle gym with a new climbing tower called Joey's Tower. Below it, there would be an open space for big art designs—and the tower would be a way to see them. Then how she would add new slides and swings. And a spice garden. "Because in India, spices are very important," she finished.

There was one thing I still didn't understand. "Why did you leave the drawing in the Advice Box for me to find it?" I asked.

Veena's eyes blinked behind their aqua frames. "Because," she said solemnly, "you are an important person like Joey. You are a leader. I knew that you would make this dream happen."

And then she folded up her drawing and handed it me.

April: Decision Time

All weekend, I went over the conversation with Veena in my head. And I thought about Joey. And the new playground idea. And what Mr. Ulysses had said about me. And rare birds.

(And I took the little girl who lives next door trick-or-treating for Halloween because her mom had to work. The girl was a ladybug, and I wore a pair of sparkly antennae.)

By Monday, I'd reached a decision.

I found Mr. Mac in his office before school started. Taking a deep breath, I told him that I wanted to quit the Buddy Bench.

"What? Why would you want to do that, April? You're doing a fantastic job with it!" the counselor said, looking totally shocked by the news. He was sitting in his office, working on his laptop and eating a donut.

I told him that Veena was much better at it than I was. "She's been handling almost everything on Wednesdays and Fridays by herself anyway," I explained. Which was true. "And she's much more patient than I am with the fourth graders. The bracelet girls are kind of driving me nuts these days."

"Really?" Mr. Mac said. "Is this something I should talk to them about?"

I shook my head. "No, I just really want Veena to have my spot now. I don't know if she would want to be in charge of my other recesses—or if you could find someone else to do them, but I'd like to give up those days too."

"Are you sure?" Mr. Mac said, still looking totally shocked.

"Yes." I nodded. "I'm sure."

It was much harder to tell the news to Veena the next time we had recess together.

At first, she thought she had done something wrong—or that I was mad at her. She started crying (good grief), which made me backtrack and question everything I'd decided to do.

"Gosh, I didn't mean to make you cry, Veena." I wrapped my arms around her shoulders and gave her a quick hug. "I'm trying to do a *good* thing," I said.

It took a lot of explaining to get Veena to see why I wanted to quit the Buddy Bench and go back to the sixth-grade lunch. And how it would help her out.

"Is it because of the boy at the football match?" Veena mumbled, brushing away more tears.

"Football *game*," I said, rolling my eyes. "No."

Veena's eyes blinked behind her glasses. "Then why?"

I took a deep breath. "It's kind of hard to describe in

words, but I guess Joey's art and everything that happened at the game made me start thinking about what I've been missing."

Veena looked down. "What do you mean?"

I took a deep breath. "Well, I was thinking about how amazing the tiger was—and how you really had to be there to see it appear on the field in front of you. And I was thinking that even though it was kind of terrifying for all of us to go to the game—for Joey and for you and for me—we did it." I smiled at Veena. "We were there."

"And then I was thinking about Joey moving away and starting over—and you coming here from India and starting over. . . ."

I paused and took another breath. "And I guess I just felt like it was time for me to try going back to being part of the sixth grade lunch again. It may be a total failure and I may totally regret it, but I want to at least try."

"Okay . . . ," Veena said, not looking convinced.

"And I was thinking that if you take over the Buddy Bench—that will help to make *you* a lot more important than me. Kids—and adults—will look up to you as a leader," I told her. "Then you'll be able to make this new playground happen." I pulled the folded drawing out of my pocket and handed it to Veena. "Seriously, it's a really good idea."

"No." Veena shook her head firmly. "I want you to make it happen."

"Nope," I told her, crossing my arms. "I can't. In less

than a year, I won't even be here. I'll be in junior high. It's up to you and the fifth graders to turn this boring old space into something beautiful." I waved my arm at the playground.

But Veena still looked upset, and I felt guilty for having caused it.

So I backtracked on my plan a little. "Okay. How about if I keep volunteering for the Buddy Bench on Wednesdays? It'll be our bonding time," I said. "We can talk to each other and catch up on everything then. And if you want me to help you with your playground project, I'll do that too," I added.

Veena's voice trembled. "So we will still be like friends?"

"We *are* friends," I said.

"All right," she said, chewing on her lip.

I glanced at the time on my phone, realizing I'd better leave before I talked myself out of everything. "Now, I've got to go inside so I don't miss lunch. You can do it." I pointed at Veena. "Remember, believe in yourself."

Then I headed inside and tried to believe in myself too.

April: Snowflakes in January

A couple of weeks after Homecoming, Ms. Getzhammer made an official announcement about Joey. She told everyone that Joey's family had moved, and unfortunately, Joey wouldn't be returning to Marshallville. By then, it didn't really matter. Most of the kids had already figured it out for themselves.

The principal promised that once she received a forwarding address for Joey, she would share the information with everyone, so kids could write letters to him.

As far as I know, an address never arrived.

However, a huge snowflake appeared on a beach in Clearwater, Florida, in January. A photo of it was featured in a lot of newspapers and news feeds. My mom saw it on Facebook. Nobody claimed responsibility for the beach snowflake, but we were convinced it was Joey's way of telling us where he had ended up.

April: What Happened Later

After Joey left, a lot of things happened to Veena and me.

Going back to sixth-grade lunch was really stressful at first, especially since everybody already had their own places and their own groups of friends. I tried to tell myself that if I could solve the mysteries of Joey, I could figure out the sixth graders—but it took time. I relied on my mind's eye a lot.

I ended up avoiding Julie Vanderbrook's group. I sat at the end of Tanner's table where Noah and Jacob and some other girls were sitting. Eventually, we kind of broke off and made our own table group.

Noah became a really good friend of mine, even though people kept asking if we were dating. We did go out for a couple of weeks, but we decided it was easier just being friends.

I invited Wally Rensbacher to sit with us at lunch a few times. Eventually, he joined our group too.

One of the most surprising people who became one of my friends was Rachel—yes, of the two Rs. Even though I had never been a big fan of the two Rs, they had been nicer to me after Homecoming. We waved at one another in the hallways and sometimes we'd sit together at school events.

Then, Rochelle's parents got divorced after Thanksgiving and she had to move away pretty suddenly with her mom. After Rochelle left, Rachel started looking worse and worse. Her hair was stringy and her face had a lot of acne all of sudden. Although she had always worn a ton of black, her arms were scribbled with black ink now. Passing by her in the hallway one day, I noticed how the front of her notebook was completely covered with black spirals of ballpoint pen.

That's when I knew she needed help.

That same week, I went over to where she was sitting by herself at a sixth-grade pizza party during our activity block. I asked her if she wanted to sit with our group.

"No," she said, at first. "That's okay. Thanks."

"Come on," I said. "I already saved a spot for you." Then I literally picked up her drink and her paper plate—which was really brave, considering that she might have socked me for doing that in the past—and I brought her over to our group.

"Rachel—meet everyone. Everyone—meet Rachel," I said, even though we all knew each other's names.

Rachel slid into the seat next to me with her head down and her hair curtained over her eyes.

Even though she wasn't in our lunch period, she sat with our group at most sixth-grade things after that—and surprisingly, she turned out to be a lot smarter and funnier than I thought. When she showed up at school in a cheerful flowered blouse and new leggings after Christmas break, people almost didn't recognize her. By spring, even her black nail polish was gone.

I also kept my promise to Veena through the rest of the school year.

Every Wednesday, I'd skip the sixth-grade lunch to sit with her on the Buddy Bench.

She had the genius idea of using Mr. Ulysses's Polaroid camera to take photos of the playground's rusted and broken equipment to hand out to our school district's administrators. The old-fashioned photos seemed to make more of an impact than showing ordinary pictures on our phones or laptops. I helped Veena do presentations for the PTA and the school board. And we met with Marshallville's mayor once.

We learned that change happens very slowly.

The design and funding for the playground renovation weren't approved until my freshman year of high school. Veena was in junior high by then. The school district and the PTA paid for new swings and a new wooden climbing structure that is named Joey's Tower, just like Veena suggested. The school added two more Buddy Benches, so there are three of them now. For more conversation.

There's a small garden and the Yoda Tree—which has grown a lot bigger.

Visitors to the school often ask about the unusual circle of white stones in the far corner of the playground. The path is shaped in a large spiral. A plaque nearby says it is called the Spiral of Deep Thinking.

The name and sign were Mr. Mac's ideas.

Veena and I tried to convince him that a lot of kids—even young kids—have to deal with sadness in their lives, but Mr. Mac thought the spiral needed to have a more positive and uplifting message for little kids. (He became the principal after Ms. Getzhammer retired.)

As it turned out, the new name didn't really catch on. Everyone kept calling it Joey's Spiral of Sadness anyway.

It is very popular.

April: What Happened (Much) Later

These days you can find spirals all over Marshallville if you know where to look. Almost every afternoon—and weekends, too—you can see kids walking around the one on Marshallville's playground, letting go of whatever sadness is inside them: loneliness, fear, rejection, losing teams, bad grades, mean kids—you name it.

There are spirals hidden in people's gardens and spirals drawn on the sidewalks of Main Street. And just last year, the city planted a beautiful spiral-shaped rose garden in the center of town. The roses are all different colors: red, pink, yellow, lavender, and—of course—orange.

Little by little, our town is finally getting more colorful.

Although it has been six years since Joey left—and I'm a senior in high school now—Joey's influence can still be found everywhere you look.

As far as we know, Marshallville High School continues to be the only high school in the nation with a Team Artist. Each pregame show always includes a chalk Tiger—some have been pretty large and impressive, although none have ever matched Joey's spectacular creation.

(Kenston is still waiting for another eagle to appear.)

We are also the site of the only Presidential Quiz Competition for Michigan high schools. Of course, Wally Rensbacher runs it.

Our football team didn't get to the playoffs during my sixth-grade year—despite the 50–0 Homecoming win—but we've been a contender nearly every year since then. Tanner Torchman is our star quarterback now. Although he's the most popular guy in high school, he always says hello to me whenever he sees me in the hallways.

Noah and I have remained best friends, and we have a whole group going to prom together this spring. Noah is wearing a vintage tuxedo and a fedora—which I think is a little over the top, but I'm not going to tell him that.

Veena is the student council president at the high school now. She was the first junior to win election. She is one hundred percent sure that she wants to go into politics someday. Or photography.

Unlike Veena, I have no clue what I want to be.

I'm the managing editor of our high school newspaper, and I'm in literary club, debate club, and theater. I take classes in Mandarin, and I tutor two kids in my neighborhood in reading. I may not be a rare bird, but I'm a really busy one.

Over the years, I've thought a lot about Joey and what he would think of Marshallville today. Would he ever come back for a visit?

One time, I swear I might have spotted him in the crowd at one of our football games. During a game last year, I just happened to look up and I saw this tall, lanky kid with blondish hair and something gold around his neck, perched at the top of our grandstand bleachers. I raced to the top.

Of course, by the time I got there, he was gone.

Veena and I often talk about the legend of Joey—that's how we refer to him. *The legend of Joey.* We wonder: How much of what we remember about him is true? And how much did he change the direction of all our lives back in sixth grade? If we hadn't noticed him, would everything be different now? Without Joey (and the Buddy Bench), would I have found the same group of friends? Would Veena be student council president? Would Marshallville have a spiral rose garden?

As Mr. Ulysses said years ago—*you can never tell where a simple line may lead.*

Sometimes when I'm feeling overwhelmed, I try to look at things the way Joey did. From above. It always makes big problems seem smaller.

Lying down also helps.

Veena and I still keep an eye out for any signs of Joey's art. When one of us spots another picture by him online or in the news, we usually call or text each other.

Sometimes we get an email message from Mr. Ulysses about it. He retired to Florida a couple of years ago and started his own company. It is called Odysseus Enterprises, and the company makes new products for schools.

He has already patented several inventions, including a universal handle for school lockers (so they won't jam) and a music-playing mop for janitors. When Mr. Ulysses emails us about Joey's art, the subject line always has these two words: *Another One.*

By now, we have a whole collection of Joey's possible designs: exquisite stars, big snowflakes, cartoon characters, elaborate labyrinths, geometric patterns, faces of famous people—even the *Mona Lisa.*

The designs have been found in many different places— from snowy fields to sandy beaches. And yes, they've appeared on quite a few school playgrounds. Sometimes Joey's name is mentioned as the artist and sometimes it isn't.

Earlier this year, an outline of Yoda appeared on a beach in England and that discovery thrilled us the most. We're convinced it was Joey's way of telling us that he had finally

made his way across the Atlantic. Hopefully, he has met up with some of the secret circle makers too.

We like to think that maybe we played a part in changing his life—or maybe we just gave him a safe place to land for a while.

But take our advice and keep watching. You just might spot a rare bird yourself someday.

Consider yourself lucky if you do.

AUTHOR'S NOTE

Can one photo inspire an entire book? Yes! The idea for this book began with this Facebook photo that caught my attention and imagination:

The "Joey Byrd" in the middle of the picture is my nephew in real life. His name is Miles, and he was the inspiration for this story. Perhaps you have a Joey Byrd in your family—someone who sees the world in a unique, one-of-a-kind way. A rare and special person.

Or maybe you are a Joey Byrd yourself.

I spent a lot a time talking to Miles to gather details and ideas for Joey's part of the story. We walked around his old elementary school playground, and he told me about his spirals of sadness and how they helped him to cope.

It was hard to hear some of his stories. Just like Joey, Miles struggled to read and write because of the way he pictured words in his mind. In elementary school, he had a tough time making friends and fitting in. That's why he started doing the playground art.

To create the character of Joey, I imagined what might have happened if Miles's art and abilities had been discovered by his school and community. How could it have changed everything?

I have met students in other schools who have similar visual-spatial gifts and can picture the world from a bird's-eye view, just like Joey and Miles. Some kids have told me how they've made spirals of sadness or playground art of their own.

The concept of creating giant works of art on land isn't a new idea—it has been around for centuries. At places like Stonehenge, prehistoric people made large stone circles, possibly for ceremonial purposes. In Wiltshire, a county in southern England, there are a number of hillsides marked with the chalk-white outlines of giant horses, like the one that Veena finds online. A few have been around for hundreds of years or longer. In fact, one known as the Uffington White Horse is believed to be more than three thousand years old. No one knows for sure why they were originally made.

In the story, Veena also discovers the artistry of crop circles, which are special designs made by flattening crops, usually cereal grasses, in fields. The formations can be perfect circles, rings, spirals—or really elaborate patterns and images. They have appeared often in fields in southern England near Stonehenge, but they've also been spotted in other places throughout the world, including the United States.

As Veena points out in the book, there are many different theories about how the crop circles are made. In England, some are made by a talented and secretive group of artists who call themselves "circlemakers." They like to recreate truly impressive, mathematically influenced designs as a way to inspire and amaze people. Other crop circles may be formed by unknown natural phenomena or as-yet-unexplained causes.

Just like Joey's creations, land art often has an aura of power and mystery—and it often leaves unanswered questions.

Once I started writing, I found even more examples of "big art." While working on the book, I met and interviewed

Marc Treanor (sandcircles.co.uk), a well-known land artist in Wales. He makes amazing works of art on the beautiful sandy beaches scattered along the west coast of Wales.

To create his art, Marc rakes wet sand into intricate designs, such as spirals and labyrinths—even realistic faces. (If you want to learn more about him, be sure to check out his breathtaking drone footage and videos on YouTube.)

He explained to me how an important part of being a land artist is being able to let go of your art—which is a hard thing to do. Sometimes the waves erase his designs soon after he finishes them. "You have to be able to leave your art and walk away," he said. "You have no control over how people will react to it or what will happen once you leave."

Which reminded me a lot of Joey.

Land artist Simon Beck creates in snow—and his work gave me the idea for Joey's snowflakes. Simon makes enormously complex designs in ski resort valleys and on alpine lakes using just his imagination—and his snowshoes, a ski pole, and a compass.

As you can probably guess, his art is physically demanding and dangerous. Some of his designs can reach the size of ten soccer fields, and they often take several days to complete. He has created valley-sized stars, snowflakes, space invaders, and geometric figures, such as Sierpiński triangles. "As time passes, naturally I run out of easy designs, so they gradually get more complex," he wrote in his book, *Simon Beck: Snow Art.*

Another artist re-creates entire cities, like New York

and Tokyo, on paper, after seeing them only briefly from a helicopter or skyscraper. The artist's name is Stephen Wiltshire. Although he was unable to speak as a young child, his visual memory is so precise and photographic, he can recall the exact number of windows on city buildings as he draws them. Check out some videos of his incredible work on his website: stephenwiltshire.co.uk.

And what is Miles up to now?

Although he no longer does big art, he's in high school, where he loves playing the trumpet in the marching band. And just like a lot of kids his age, he's learning to drive. He's also a fan of vinyl records and vintage cars—and, especially, historical stuff.

In other words, he's getting along okay and finding his own place in the world, like the fictional character of Joey.

Miles once told me, "Different kids, like me, have to use our creativity to escape trouble."

I loved that idea.

This book is for you, Miles—and for all the Joey Byrds out there.

ACKNOWLEDGMENTS

There aren't enough Buddy Benches for all the buddies who played a part in this book. Special thanks to my editor, Nancy Siscoe, and my agent, Steven Malk, for helping me to see the lines in the wood chips. I'm grateful to artist Xingye Jin for Joey's views from above and to reader Jyotsna Sreenivasan for her Veena advice. A massive hug to the women of Stanford House 2018: Rebecca Barnhouse, Megan Whalen Turner, Cinda Williams Chima, and Tricia Springstubb—all amazing authors who kept me going through the toughest parts. And thanks to Gene Benedetto for being there when I needed it.

Big thanks to Phil, Ina, and Matt Guzman, who were the very first to read the finished book! Much gratitude to teacher Courtney Rubino and her sixth graders, who provided so many of April's details for the story, including green chickens. Special thanks to these sixth graders who volunteered to be first draft editors: Natalee Confere, Madalyn Burgdorf, and Ava Sabatucci. And thanks to the Eagle-Eyed Editors of Mrs. Calaway's Team 511–512 who read the final draft so carefully and shaped the ending of the book.

Finally, thanks to Mom, Marcy, Mike, Miles, and Ethan—and the rest of my family near and far—for all the support and love that made this book possible. I promise no cattail pancakes for dinner tonight.